# MANICURES & MAYHEM

## BEAUTIFUL BEASTS ACADEMY

MILA YOUNG

KIM FAULKS

*This one is for the fans, for sticking with us and jumping onboard with both feet for this crazy ass ride. For our families, for understanding when we're tired and grumpy, and feeding us chocolate in the hopes it'll soothe the savage beast. And for our phenomenal edits, and proofreaders, you guys are the absolute best.*

*Mila: To Kim - thanks for making me laugh so much and having the whackiest ideas. Love Mila.*

*Kim: To Mila, you are so easily led. Mwahahaha...seriously, you are the best damn co-writer. Just keep saying yes...*

*And lastly, to the muse, Hekate. When we need a second wind, you are always there. Thank you, I think you'll enjoy this one.*

Grab your FREE
book and start
the Beautiful
Beasts Academy
Series today!

***Welcome to Beautiful Beasts Academy, where the only thing more dangerous than the haunted grounds are the students themselves.***

Life as the daughter of the city's most prominent Vampire
was tough enough.
Bodyguards with fangs.
Paparazzi everywhere I turn.
Dates with an overbearing Demon.
I hated it all. So when the opportunity to attend Academy
reared its head, I jumped at the chance.
I could hide there, blend in with all the other beautiful
beasts and try to ignore my bodyguard.

I wanted normal
I craved boring.

But fate has a shitty sense of humor, way worse than mine.
So when I find a body in the middle of my bedroom on my
first night there...I'm not threatened not with
death...something worse.

Getting expelled.

And to prove my innocence I have to find the real killer in a
school full of monsters.

# CHAPTER ONE

## DO NOT EMBARRASS THY FAMILY NAME

CRYSTAL GLASSES CLINKED. DIAMONDS SPARKLED. Heads were thrown back in raucous laughter. But it was all fake. Every single thing here. Fake smiles. Fake alliances. Everyone at this goddamn party would bury a knife to the hilt in the person they sat next to...*or a set of fangs.*

And I didn't care. The threat of death was a joke here...to most of us at least.

It's what happened when you were the most powerful Vampire family in the city.

I sat at the table in the center of the room, bored, counting the carats in Glorian's ring across the table and then sighed. Anything under ten was considered lowly at these dinners, and she was sporting a measly five.

Pity.

I kinda liked her.

The others at this dinner would eat her alive...and if you think I was kidding...*I wasn't.*

She wasn't mortal, so it wasn't against the pact. Still, all the killing and the biting bored me to tears. I just wanted to be normal. To have a normal boyfriend, and a normal family. Instead I got this...this shitshow which was my life.

"Hermond," Mom cried out as the dark blur slid through the glitz and the glamor. She rose from the table, clutching the train of her body hugging blood red chiffon dress.

I grabbed the dagger we used as cutlery and spun the sharpened blade on the table. The tip stopped at the same mark...once...twice...twenty fucking times. God I was bored.

"Over here!" Mom called stilling my hand. I lifted my head to see the most powerful Vampire in the city. He was the reason we were here...he was the reason for this whole thing tonight.

I scanned the packed tables of the gala, catching all heads turn, especially my father's, and felt my stomach sink. Panic sent a shiver through that undead thing in the middle of my chest. I scanned for a way out...to slip between Dad's four close protection bodyguards and the pain in the ass Demon who was always one step behind him, like a goddamn lap dog.

That particular Demon turned his head, dark eyes glinting with power-hungry madness and smiled at me. I swallowed a shudder and forced a smile.

Thorin. *Ugh.*

He'd been trying to get me on my own all night. Greedy hands sliding along my thigh, sulphur-foul breath whispering all kinds of sick shit in my ear. *Power.* The kind that made him hard and me cringe.

"I'm deeply honored you could make it," Mom gushed to the head Vamp and reached for his hand.

Her pale skin almost sparkled under the overhead lights.

*Keep your head down. Don't make eye contact.*

*Maybe they'll leave me out of it...pretend I'm not here.*

The tip of the silver dagger slowly spun, coming to a stop, pointed at me. I shifted on my seat, sliding my ass lower. Maybe I could just slip under the table? No one would know I was gone.

"I'd love to introduce you to my daughter."

I stilled and inwardly groaned with those words. I tried to ignore them. Pretend I didn't hear her. *Yeah, good call.* I was a statue. I wasn't here.

Until she cleared her throat.

Energy danced along my skin like the sting of a thousand ants. I sucked in a breath (for effect really) and then forced myself to rise with a fake ass smile on my lips.

I met the Vampire's stare and swallowed the harsh bark of laughter. He was a walking goddamn cliché; long raven black hair cascading along his shoulders, ending in a widow's peak in the middle of his forehead.

Cold, dead eyes stared at me as he lowered his head in a small bow and lifted his hand, the *monstrous* red jewel hanging like a goddamn tumor in the middle of his finger. I winced at the sight. I was expected to lower my head, an inch lower than his and kiss...*that.*

My stomach rolled with the thought. Still the Vampire waited.

If we were the most powerful Vampires in the city, then this dude was the most powerful across the eastern seaboard. *Don't do it.* My stomach clenched in warning, and acid reached higher along the back of my throat.

Mom's dress shifted. Pain cut across my shin, with a sharp kick from Mom.

If I had to do this shit...*I was doing it once.* I closed my eyes, praying I didn't coat his precious clan ring with tonight's dinner, and pressed my lips. Anger mingled with a burst of retribution. I lifted my head, meeting the Vampire's gaze. "Nice to meet you. My name's Weiner Livingstone."

"Weiner? Isn't that a..." The Vamp boss shot a look of disgust at Mom.

"*No!*" Mom cried out, stuttering. Her eyes widened as she barged me aside. A high pitched bark of maniacal laughter broke free. "She means Morwenna. *Ha! Weiner,* always joking. Aren't you, *Morwenna?*"

Mom cut a steely gaze toward me.

*Damage control.*

I was in so much trouble.

I smiled sweetly and caught the shake of the Vampire's head. "If that's all you need from me, Mom?"

"*Yes,*" she answered fast. "That *will* be all."

And with a slow nod I stepped away. Limped, actually and winced, fighting the urge to reach down and rub my shin. Mom sure had one helluva kick.

"Mor." Thorin stepped close.

He glanced at Mom as she turned to him. There seemed to be an unspoken conversation between them I wasn't privy to. Didn't matter. I'd done enough for tonight.

"What the Hell do you think you're playing at?" Thorin fell in step and snarled in my ear.

"Not playing at anything," I growled softly and worked my way through the battleground of the Immortal elite, putting as much distance between him and me as possible

"Mor! Mor, can we get a close up?" screamed a paparazzi from the edge of the cordoned off area.

The flare of a flash followed, camera shutters snapped. The glare, blinding. The family ring on my finger encased me with a kind of enchantment that held my reflection in a mirror and made me appear in photographs.

I winced and turned my head as the thunder of footsteps followed. There was a shout and then a scuffle and the hunter with a camera was gone.

"Are you okay?" Thorin slid his hands along my arms, trying his best to pull me against his chest, and pretend he cared.

I shoved my splayed hand against the hard swell of his muscles and shoved away. "Of course, I'm fine. This is my damn life, isn't it...all on fucking display."

"What's got into you?" he snarled and cast a panicked gaze across the rest of the party behind us.

He didn't understand me. Didn't even like me really. All he saw was my name...Morwenna Livingstone, daughter of the royal line...heir to all *this*...

But I didn't want it.

*None of it.*

Thorin's fingers dug into the flesh of my arm, grinding against bone as he tried to pull me closer. I scanned the others, searching for a way out of this damn mess and caught the red eyes of a Goblin. They were all here...anyone who was anyone.

*Except for the Wolves.*

There was no way they'd be invited. Our clan hated them above than any other immortal, especially Dad. So fucking pretentious. I'd set fire to it all if I could.

"Nothing," I snarled and shoved away from the boyfriend I never wanted.

*We need to look perfect, Morwenna,* Dad's words rang inside my head. *We need to look every bit as powerful as we are. Power breeds power, and you my darling daughter are the envy of every Vampire girl in the city...no, in the clan.*

I stumbled away from the laughter and the murmured voices, shoved away from the steel grip around my arm.

Still, he haunted my steps as I made for the open French doors to our home.

"You can't leave the party. We haven't been seen together," Thorin growled.

I reached up, yanked the small diamond tiara from the top of my head and winced at the sting as strands of my hair tore free. "Stand there with your dick in your hand for all I care."

"You really are a bitch," he growled, his eyes darkening.

I stilled, narrowed my gaze, and then slowly turned. "You know, that's probably the most honest thing you've ever said to me. Congratulations for finally finding your balls."

And then I left him behind, taking long strides to get away from him and the stench of Hell as fast as I could. I turned at the foyer and raced along the carpeted marble stairs to the third floor, then made for the south wing. Servants waited at the head of every level, hands folded, heads bowed. Vampires. All of them. Slaves to my father, but still vampires.

"Mistress," Helene murmured and stepped forward. "May I assist you tonight?"

It wasn't a question. It was *never a question*. It was a plea.

I gave a nod and listened to the soft thud of her footsteps behind me as I strode into my wing and made for my bedroom. My bathroom was on one side, an expansive robe crammed with Prada and Gucci, and a glass cupboard for every expensive handbag in the world.

It was a wardrobe to make a Sheik's daughter weep with envy.

And a wardrobe that would feed the entire homeless a thousand times over.

But still it wasn't enough according to my parents.

There was always one more dress, one more hand-bag...one more token of just how perfect we were supposed to look.

I reached behind my back for the zipper, and strode toward the ornate dresser and matching seat.

"Mistress." Helene's fingers gently replaced my own, working the pearl buttons first before her deft hands worked the hidden zipper and I stepped out of the Oscar de la Renta masterpiece designed especially for this night.

"I shouldn't have provoked them tonight," I murmured and lifted my gaze to Helene's careful expression. "I embarrassed them."

"Your parents love you, Mistress."

It was the only answer I'd get, even if it was wrong. For once I wish I had someone to give it to me straight, to shove when I pushed. Someone who didn't care that my father was the equivalent to the head of the Vampire mob. But someone who saw *me*. The real me. I lifted my hand and fingered the hand stitched ornate brasserie—and *not all this*.

The dress slipped free and crumpled to the floor at my feet. I stepped out, in nothing but silk underwear, and then sat at the stool, reaching down to unhook the clasp on my heels.

"Would Mistress like her goat's milk bath tonight?"

I shook my head. "No, thank you. Not tonight."

Helene bent and plucked my dress from the floor, and then disappeared into the wardrobe. Overhead lights sparkled just like the stars at midnight. Dad had them mapped out, each tiny light sparkling for me. It'd been a gift when I turned ninety-nine.

I couldn't wait for the day I turned a hundred, it'd be the party of a lifetime.

It'd take another four hundred years until I hit the prime of my life.

Then I'd be unstoppable.

I slid my heels from my feet and massaged my arches. Faint laughter echoed all the way to my wing from outside. I'd not hear from them tonight.

I unhooked my bra and slid my fingers into the edge of my panties as Helene walked from the wardrobe. There wasn't a blink as I stepped free and strode toward the bed naked. She'd seen me this way ever since I was born.

A tiny ache burned across the inside of my upper arm as I grasped the negligee draped over the end of my bed. A small bruise was already rising to the surface. Three small marks in the shape of Thorin's fingers. The bastard was lucky I didn't nail his ass to the damn wall with a cross. I wonder what Daddy dearest would say if he saw these. I doubted Thorin would be his favorite for long.

But the marks would be gone in the morning.

Along with the memory of every embarrassing thing I said tonight.

Just like it always was.

Helene picked up my panties and bra as I slipped on the negligee and crawled into the fresh silk sheets. I slid a hand under the pillow next to mine and pulled out the white tablet. I didn't want to be out there with their hierarchy and greed. I wanted to be with friends.

I hit the button and the screen came to life. My fingers danced across the glass, and then the cheeky smile from Luke Perry appeared.

"Oh Dylan, why can't you be real?" I whispered as Helene dimmed the lights and slipped from my bedroom.

Crystal glasses clinked before a faint scream echoed for a second and then was cut short.

Looked like they finally had enough of Glorian's five carat ring and her broke ass betraying family. But I didn't care, not when I stared into Dylan's eyes and lost myself in Beverly Hills 90210.

<hr>

"ARE YOU PROUD OF YOURSELF, MORWENNA?"

I winced at the sound of my name when Dad used it like that. "It depends, should I be, Daddy?"

He lifted his gaze from his desk and seized mine. He was pissed, more than normal. "You embarrassed your Mother last night. Hermond is a powerful ally, one we desperately need."

There was an edge in his voice, one I hadn't heard before. A flare of concern cut through my center. "Daddy...is everything okay?"

He smiled, but it was a forced a smile. *He was never fake with me.* "We are, but we can't afford another stunt like last night, do you understand me? We have to be careful and always watching each other's backs. It's why I was hoping not to have to entertain..."

He cast a quick gaze to an envelope in the middle of his desk. It was the fifth time he looked at the damn thing. "Daddy?"

Gold sparkled as he reached across the desk. The soft filtered ray of sunlight hit his hand. There was a small sizzle, and the faint stench of burning flesh before the power of his ring held the danger of the sun at bay.

The rings on our hands meant we could be out during the day, but it didn't always stop the burn, not when we were tired...or when we were sick...*and Dad didn't look tired.* Fear gripped like a fist, fingers clenching tight like steel bands across my chest. "Daddy, are you sick?"

There wasn't even a second before he answered, a fraction of a second really, but for the most powerful, most influential Vampire in the city, and my father—it was *far* too long.

"No, I'm fine. But I need to talk to you. We have a responsibility as Livingstone's, one that unfortunately has landed on your young shoulders."

"I'm not *that* young," I muttered.

He just chuckled and shook his head. "Nevertheless, we have to show the rest of the world we take the pact seriously—even if it's on the surface. I was hoping to keep this from our door. Hell knows I didn't want this for you, but it seems after last night's antics there's no room to ignore the command of my superiors. You embarrassed me last night, and not only that, you brought the entire clan under scrutiny. So, my hand's been forced on this one. There's a school for the children of the most influential immortal families."

He didn't want this for me?

Lightning coursed through my chest.

The undead muscle in my chest gave a small *throb*.

"A school where *we* as a family will be watched. Every word *and* every action will be weighed and measured by those far more powerful than me. You'll have to leave us, for a while at least. You'll have to leave Thorin, and all the things you love..."

His voice melted into nothing. All I could see was a school where I was Brenda...and I had a chance at being *normal. "I'lldoit!"*

Dad flinched and stilled, mouth agape, halfway through a sentence where he'd have to talk me into leaving this life behind. "You'll do it? Don't you want to take some time to think about it at least?"

I cut my gaze to the envelope, catching the elegant crawl on the front and shook my head. "What's to think about? You need me to do this, right?"

He gave a slow nod...as though he was suddenly unsure of all this.

My Dad.

My powerful, deadly as fuck Dad...was unsure about sending his little girl to a school full of strangers. I gave him the sweetest smile I could and inwardly screamed with excitement. "I'll be a good girl...*I promise.*"

# CHAPTER TWO

## MAKE FRIENDS AND NOT ENEMIES

Darkness permeated every inch of the family armored limousine.

But it wasn't bullets my family cared about.

It was the sun.

Every possible gap was sealed tight, luckily breathing for us was optional. I flopped into the back seat, the leather groaning beneath me. A week had passed since the gala event, and Dad agreed to send me to the Academy. Seven days of waiting. 168 hours of counting down. And here I was, bags in the trunk, ready, but still...something felt off.

The black window tint blocked out 99% of the sun's rays, but it didn't block out the movement of Mom's frantic waving. Dad stood with his hands folded over his chest, holding his emotions in check. Like always. Dickhead Thorin lingered like an unwanted lump, farewelling me only because it was expected of him.

But we all knew the truth.

Even Dad.

Thorin pretended to like me for the sake of family and

greed; mostly greed, and I was the sucker jammed in the middle of that fucked up sandwich.

Unease stirred in my gut again. I'd dreamed of moving out of home for decades. Countless reruns of 90210 and Pretty Little Liars fueled every fantasy.

So why was I worried now?

I attending all family functions like the good Vampire. I had no friends, unless Daddy approved, not that there was anyone outside the back-stabbing, vein puncturing girls who moved in certain circles. And there was no way I was dealing with that.

"You ready for this?" A voice came from the darkness.

Chuck leaned forward, and I sensed his concern. Ice Pick others called him, but not me. To me he was Chuck, my bodyguard...my friend. But he had a reputation to uphold, so Ice Pick it was, given to himself for driving an ice pick into his victims on every kill, right before he bit through the side of their neck. And I'd bet my kickass stiletto Manolo Blahnik black boots I'd find his weapon of choice somewhere in this limo if I checked.

But I honestly didn't care. Half the time I assumed the muscle in the Immortal elite gang made up their own name to sound terrifying. No idea why, when Dad's name alone sent the fear of death into most people; immortal or otherwise.

Yep, lots of death and blood in my past.

But not my future. That, I was determined to change.

If it was up to me, I'd change my name to Brenda, be an ordinary girl, and catch a bus to the Academy without drawing attention. Dad would be mortified.

Only I had a shadow...*Chuck.*

The Vampire had been with me for as long as I remembered. A warrior from the Nightcore clan, he was more my father than Dad ever was. He'd attended every birthday party, every defense class, and even my first aid lesson for vamps. On my thirteenth birthday, Dad forgot to get me a present, not that I'd needed one, but Chuck was sweet enough to give me something in secret. A thigh strap for stealthily carrying a blade. I loved it because Dad would disapprove. If Chuck had a beating heart, it'd be made of gold.

"Do I have a choice?" I replied through the dark, the speakers delivering my response to the driver's compartment out front, where he sat with the driver.

"You always have a choice, Morwenna."

I groaned under my breath, turning the gold ring on my middle finger, the power rushing through me. It pricked along my arms like ants biting my flesh.

"Then I guess I'm ready," I added with a sigh.

We pulled away from the curb. I glanced back at my parents and waved, but felt stupid because they couldn't see me. Lowering my hand, I slouched into the seat.

Yep, this was happening. New start. No more dull parties. Hell, I was going to love living at this school and leaving all my baggage behind. I'd be normal here. Make new friends, and have fun for a change. I fidgeted in my seat, ready and pumped. Just like in 90210, I'd fall into the role of Brenda at the Academy with my gang of friends. I'd find my Dylan, and I pictured my favorite episode of the Spring Dance with Dylan deciding who to ask to the dance. Of course, he'd select me.

The first time my aunty, Lentua had come to visit us all the way from Romania, she got me hooked on the show. Apparently, she streamed the series in her castle...yep you heard right...and she got me addicted, even if it wasn't the *in* thing. I didn't care. For me, it was the epitome of the life I longed to experience.

Close to two hours later and three pit stops for the bathroom, we veered off the freeway. I'd drank two bags of blood this morning, to keep myself full for the day and night, but the stuff went right through me.

When we slowed down, butterflies somersaulted in my stomach, and I opened my window with the press of a button. Fresh air washed through my dark hair, driving it over my shoulders. The air was rich with the fragrance of freshly cut lawn and dampness. Sunlight pinched my skin, and I squinted against the brightness, but the sting faded just as quickly as it started with the power of the ring on my finger.

We drove down a two-lane, winding road, past an open field. A dense forest lay in the distance, so dark, the light seemed to have vanished within its grasp. It stretched out in every direction like an ocean.

Soon enough, we passed a lofty, stone wall that stretched out the length of the grounds. My knees bounced as I spied the arched entrance and pebbled driveway.

We turned into it, the school name, Bestias Academy, was chiseled in stone near the entrance, worn and aged. I remembered the sign from my internet search, having learned the word meant beast in Latin.

Wrought-iron gates lay open as our black limousine glided through and guided us along a driveway to the Academy. Perfectly manicured lawn spread out across the property. We approached an oversized, baroque-style stone building with clusters of sculptured winged creatures perched on the roof's corners. The place could pass for an old church. Twisted columns at the front flanked a small set of white stairs leading to a set of grand doors made of rich, mahogany. Ivy clung to the edges of the walls.

The building had that rich old-money feel to it, but also a touch of the macabre.

Totally my vibe.

I'd spent the past week researching the school. Attendees came by invite only, so I guessed I ought to feel privileged. Or maybe it was another, *don't upset the Head Vampire in town, so we better invite her daughter,* pity party. At least it wasn't an old asylum, or death row prison.

Yay. It was just a boring old school.

Bestias Academy...

Originally, it'd been built for training boys to control their beast side.

Now it just housed beasts...

We came to a dead stop, and unease crawled through my insides again. When Chuck appeared at my door and opened it, the feeling clenched tighter, and I knew what I felt.

I'd never been on my own, so what if I didn't fit in? Didn't pass the classes and got kicked out. Didn't make Dad proud and became another disappointment to him.

Then I'd be forced back home to marry demonic dicknose, Thorin.

And I was better than that. I wanted to so much more out of life...not quite sure what yet, but it wasn't to follow in the family footsteps of knocking off other vampire clans.

So, I lifted my chin, swallowed back the uncertainty and readied to make my time at Bestias Academy work, whatever it took.

I climbed out into the bright sun, and already the first threads of a headache webbed through my skull. In front of the doors was a woman dressed in a tight pencil skirt which fell to her knees, matching red heels, and a white button up shirt, tucked and cinched in around her tiny waist. Short cropped blond hair parted at the side, the longer strands tucked behind her ears. She stood, her hands held behind her back, waiting steadily. When I met her pale blue eyes, the color of the sky, she smiled, and lines curled around the corners of her mouth, showing the age she otherwise concealed so well. So, she was the welcoming party. Only one person, which I appreciated. No making a big deal, and already I liked this place.

"Quickly, this way, Morwenna." Chuck scanned the entrance and building behind him before he waved me forward, but a camera's flash from across the limo caught my attention.

Chuck's face darkened and he bared his fangs, hissing at the two paparazzi who must have driven in after us. They rushed back into their sedan and raced away.

But they got their shots of the Vampire girl's first day at a new school, and it'd be all over the social feeds in a couple of hours. I was convinced the paparazzi worked for Satan, as they appeared everywhere, following me like a bad smell.

The driver was collecting my bags from the trunk, along with an oversized duffle bag he swung over a shoulder. "That's not mine," I called out.

But when the driver met Chuck's gaze, the guard gave him the approving nod to continue.

My world spun, as my hopes and dreams faded away, and the rerun of all the episodes of Beverly Hills 90210 in my head, switched off. Chuck took a step closer, and I froze. "Wait. You're not..."

"You're the only heir to the Livingstone Empire, what do you think?" He cocked a brow.

"Oh, Hell." I clenched my jaw because this was my

chance to start fresh. How could I make new friends with him shadowing me everywhere?

"I promise to blend into the background. You won't even know I'm here." He tried to smile, and all I could see were fangs and the tattoo that covered half of his face telling every immortal who saw him how much of a badass he was.

I stared at his seven-foot towering muscled frame, and shook my head. "I doubt that. I doubt that very much."

"This way," the woman said, her voice delicate as a bird's song. She opened the door and waved us inside.

I sucked in a calming breath. I could do this.

Warmth greeted us as we stepped into a grand marble hallway, with an elaborate chandelier overhead, dripping in crystals. Ahead, the stairs twisted in a perfect spiral upward. I expected something a lot grander, textured wallpaper or something, but the walls were plain cream, and covered in paintings of old people I didn't recognise. Had to be teachers from the school. Everything looked pristine and new, unlike the exterior.

There was no one else around either, and the lady in red heels click clacked in a hurried walk to the first door on her right.

Chuck nudged me forward with a hand on my lower back while he collected our bags from the driver, so I followed her into a large office overlooking the grounds outside. An oak desk stole most of the room, the walls draped in shelves filled with books. The aroma of sandalwood wafted in the room.

"Hello Morwenna. Welcome to Bestias Academy, your new home for this year. Sorry for the informal greeting outside, but we don't normally create a grand entrance for new students. Most prefer to come in quietly."

I shook my head, almost laughing at the irony that she assumed I wanted a grand entrance. "No, this is perfect."

"Good. Take a seat." She rounded the table and I slid into the chair across from her, and only then did I notice her name on the table. Principal Briar Stone.

She collected a bunch of papers and handed them over to me along with a pen. "Due to your last minute acceptance, we ran out of time to send the paperwork for your attendance. Just something small, so we have all your contact details on hand should any emergencies arise, any medical conditions we should be aware of, and agreeing that should anything happen to you during your stay, you take full responsibility and we're not liable."

She laughed nervously, which I guessed had more to do with my dad's wrath should anything happen to me. "I've already arranged payment with your father, and I have your dorm ready, along with class schedule. Your father has informed me about your ability to enjoy the sun along with your...meal requirements."

I sat there, the pen in my hand trembling because everything was suddenly happening fast...too fast. I felt small and lost and overwhelmed. I normally did my own thing, but this here was different. I'd been homeschooled most of my life, only the best tutors teaching me everything from Latin, to piano, to trigonometry.

But this seemed too sudden and real. What if I choked and failed?

The principal's gaze settled heavily on me, along with the pressure to sign everything just to get out of her office. The walls seemed to close in around me. Was I sweating? What was wrong with me?

I flipped through the pages, scanning the words, but my head floated in the clouds, stringing together two words seemed impossible. I shook my head and searched for the line at the bottom of the page and signed each one. It came out scribbly, but I couldn't work out why this room had me so shaken.

Ms. Stone rambled on about the layout of the grounds and kept piling a mountain of things for me to review. Maps. Timetables. Wait, where did she say the blood bank was located on the property?

Perspiration rolled down my spine. How could I ever feel at home here when one room had me needing to run outside for fresh air?

"We've set your bodyguard up in a house nearby. He can't reside in the dorm so close to the students. I hope you understand."

I glanced up, finding my voice. "In all honesty, I'd rather he didn't stay here at all."

But Ms. Stone's expression fell. "Those are your father's rules."

I nodded, realizing even far away from my family, Dad would control my life. Hell.

By the time I finished, the principle marched to the door as if she couldn't wait to get me out of her office and opened the door. "Your dorm is located behind this building, follow the path to the right. It's dorm 2A"

Collecting the papers from her table, I marched outside to where Chuck waited, and he stared down at the pile in my hands with the list of teachers, their photos, and what class they taught.

"Don't worry," he said. "They're clean." He stared at the printout of their faces in my grasp.

The Principal cleared her throat and clicked her heels together. "Okay, you have today to settle in, and tomorrow morning classes start. Just remember, being on time is a sign of respect. I'll let you find your room and follow you in a moment to make sure you're settled."

I looked back at her and smiled. "Thank you."

She nodded and retreated to her desk while I headed outside. No limousine in sight, so if I got cold feet, I couldn't just run, and I noted the front gates were now closed.

I turned back to the Principal, and supressed a shudder. "Something's strange about her."

"Don't worry, we vetted her as well," was all Chuck said as we followed the path, him carrying all the bags. "You're safe."

Around the back of the building, the path spread out in three directions and clusters of buildings dotted the property amid trees and greenery. A beautiful landscape, so different to the polluted city; maybe it wouldn't be so bad here. Following the path to the right, Chuck pointed to a small shack that belonged in a fairytale, situated near a forest, complete with a chimney. "That's me over there I'm guessing."

"You'll be all right in there, Papa Smurf?" I cut him a side glance, before sniggering to myself.

He didn't bite back and kept walking alongside me.

When we reached the front door of my dorm, I tugged on the handle, but it didn't budge. "What the hell?" I rattled it again, when Chuck dropped the bag he carried by my feet and collected a keyring and key from under the top paper in my pile, then opened the door for me.

"At your service, Smurfette," he growled the words.

When he stepped inside, I grabbed his arm. "You can't go in there. The principal told me you weren't allowed." Okay, I fibbed, but if he was going to stay on campus, I needed my space.

He grumbled under his breath and I smirked as he

retreated. "At least let me carry your bags to your room." He hissed the words through clenched teeth.

I shook my head and tucked the papers under an arm, then picked up my two bags. "I'll take it from here."

Without looking back, I fumbled past the narrow doorway and let the glass door shut behind me with a bang. With a nod to Chuck through the window, I headed down the corridor with strange violet wallpaper, glancing down at my keyring in my hand. 202.

I swung toward the carpeted steps and dragged my bags. I glanced back to see Chuck still standing outside, watching me through the glass door as I struggled, his hands folded over his chest. Bastard.

I straightened my back and followed the curve of the steps, my bags banging into my legs, but I kept going to show Chuck I had this. And I moved fast too, despite the strain in my arms.

Before careening around the next corner, I glanced back to find Chuck gone. Thank hell. I spun around the corner at the top of the stairs, hauling forward one of the beastly suitcases, the momentum sending it forward. Except someone emerged from the corner at the same moment, and the case slammed into their knees.

"Fuck!" A guy with the darkest hair grunted and reeled backward, arms flailing. He stumbled over his feet, before his back hit the wall, and he gasped for air.

"Oh, shit!" I rushed over, arms outstretched to help catch him. "I'm so sorry."

His was pulling down on his tee which had ridden half way up his stomach, and I reached over and helped him cover that ribbed, tight stomach. Damn, he had muscles.

But he smacked my hands away. 'What the hell are you carrying in there? A dead body?"

I stumbled back as he fixed his clothes. "Just clothes and shoes."

When I glanced up at him, he was sniffing the air, his nose creasing, and giving me a death glare.

A rumble rolled in his chest as if detecting what I was. "Watch it, Vamp." He growled, and his eyes shifted to wolf ones—gray as the dirtiest clouds—and right then, I knew exactly who or what I was dealing with.

The hairs on my neck bristled.

Having him glare as if I were a speck on his shoes had me boiling with fury. Many races hated Vampires, but I'd never faced the racism first hand. Homeschooled remember? But the shifter in front of me grated on my nerves, and if there was one enemy Dad loathed above all others, the wolf packs gained that top spot.

"*Ugh*, Dogs belong outside!" I snapped disgusted.

His lips curled, white canines bared. Was that meant to scare me? I snatched my bags from the ground, lifted my chin, and turned away from him in a fluster.

And walked straight into a pillar.

Pain flared through my brow. I stumbled backwards.

*Who the fuck put that there?*

The sharp crack of laughter flooded my ears. I decided right then; I loathed that fur ball.

# CHAPTER THREE

WEALTH IS NOT DEFINED BY POSSESSIONS

"You've got to be kidding, right?"

I stared at the key in my hand and then the number on the door.

Footsteps sounded behind me, and I whirled to find Principal Stone stepping up to the doorway. She gave the room a scan. "Is there a problem?"

I turned to the thick cobwebs crowding the corner of the room. "Only that." And then the inch thick dust along the windowsill, and stopped at the other bed jammed up against the wall on the other side of the room. "And *that*."

I spun, eyeing the Principal. "I wasn't told I'd be sharing. *I don't share.*"

I stilled at the open door to a small bathroom, and thanked the Ancients for small mercies. At least I don't have to share.

She just held my gaze and smiled. "Don't worry Ms. Livingstone. That bed has been unoccupied for the last year. I doubt you'll be sharing with anyone."

"And the...*dirt?*" I stifled my revulsion. "What will you do about that?"

"*I* won't be doing anything Ms. Livingstone. This isn't the Hilton, we don't have maids here. But you're welcome to the mop and bucket in the cleaning closet at the end of the hall."

My damn eye twitched at the thought. A mop wouldn't be anywhere near enough. "I'll have to burn it."

"I beg your pardon?" Principal Stone took a step inside with her heels and tight pencil-straight skirt, clearly standing out in this room. I suspected her accommodation was glamorous compared to this dusty space that could easily be mistaken for a dingy motel room.

"Nothing," I muttered and gave her the perfect Livingstone smile, as fake as this entire set up.

This was no school for the elite. This was a damn prison...and I just walked into it in my goddamn Gucci shoes. I stared at the tiny wardrobe against the wall...and when I say tiny...I mean *tiny*. It wouldn't even hold the contents of one of my suitcases.

I stepped closer as Principal Stone murmured, "It'll take a little getting used to, but give it time. I promise Bestias Academy will feel like home in no time."

Footsteps echoed a second later. But I didn't bother to look over my shoulder to see her gone. I was too busy mentally preparing myself for the horror waiting within. My hand trembled as I reached for the handle. In my head I counted down; *three, two...one,* and then yanked.

There were wire hangers.

*Actual wire hangers.*

And the ugliest damn uniform I'd ever seen.

I gagged at the smell of moth balls and turned away from the vile thing, and then turned back, reaching up to unhook the hanger and pull the skirts and the shirts out into the open.

They still had the tags on the end, creases along the sides, and the skirt was almost long enough to touch my damn knees.

What the hell kind of place was this? A convent?

But the wardrobe was the icing on this cheap cotton polyester nightmare. There was no way in Hell I was putting my clothes in *that*. I stared at the suitcases near the doorway and took a step backwards until my calves hit the steel frame of the bed.

I'd made the wrong decision.

*A very wrong decision.*

I wanted to take it back, to return home where Helene was waiting along with the other maids to clean and primp and fluff. My cell phone dug into my thigh as I moved and for a second, I wanted to reach down and grasp the damn thing.

One call was all it'd take, three tiny words...*take...me...home*...and I'd be whisked out of here, and on my way back to the parties and the panicked gazes, back to fake smiles and the empty conversations. Back to being a Livingstone.

But here there was none of that.

I glanced at the corner of the room, sure there were cobwebs, but there was also potential. I could make friends here...apart from the foul mutt in the hallway outside. I bet they were just desperate for someone like me, someone with class and sophistication, someone who understood the intricacies of the many immortal races.

They were desperate for me...

I lifted the class schedule in my hand. My first class wasn't until ten am tomorrow. *Mock Hunt? What the Hell is that...some kind of new Gelato?* A shiver raced along my spine. I'd expected dance classes, training on party conversations, along with some etiquette on handling humans. Instead, I had classes on history, rituals, and combat. What the hell! Maybe I'd been wrong to think the Academy would be easy and fun.

I looked back up to my room. It needed fixing, but I had plenty of time to get this cleaned up. I gave a nod and steeled my spine. I'd make this place my bitch within a week.

"Cleaning closet," I muttered, even saying the words I felt dirty and scanned the hallway. There was a door at the end of the hall. That had to be it. I scanned the closed doors of the rooms next to mine and strode toward the damn thing, before I reached out and grasped the handle.

The lock held with a *thud*. I could force it, shear the steel...and maybe break a nail in the process. I jerked my hand away at the thought and then turned. It didn't matter.

Within a week they'd be giving me their room anyway, knock the wall down in the middle and *voila*, I'd have a walk in closet once more.

I strode to the end of the hallway and peered at the wording on the door. *Stairs*. "Not a cleaning closet, Mor."

I spun and strode back the way I came, until I passed my open door and headed to the door at the end and glanced left. There were rows and rows of rooms up here, and more the level higher. Stony walls had that chilly feel, throwing shadows in the corners. I found the door marked *Cleaning* and turned the handle.

The sharp scent of antiseptic made me gag. I reached up, pinched my nose and scanned the space before dragging a broom and dustpan free. I couldn't believe I was doing this, stooping to things like cleaning and fussing. Still I ground my jaw and carried the equipment back to the room and set to work.

First, the corners. I swept and moved things around, watching my nails as I shoved the vacant bed aside and cleaned around the corners. For a second, I thought about the old occupant. Maybe she detested cleaning as well?

And after producing a film of sweat on my brow I stood back and admired my magic.

The place was clean...not spotless like home, but no cobwebs, no dust...no mothballs, or wire hangers. I felt good, fueled with purpose as I carried the dustpan back to the cleaning closet and shoved the door closed before I yanked my phone from my pocket.

*Chuck, I need my hangers. I cannot deal with the wire ones here. Can you please have my padded, scented hangers, and my silk sheet sent to my room...Oh, and some of those delicious blood muffins Clare makes...Kisses, M.*

I hit send and then strode back to my room and the first suitcase, dragging it over to the bed. One heave and the thing landed with a *thump*. I worked the zipper, revealing silks and Armani shoes. I packed what I could into the now dusted shelves and stowed the half filled suitcase next to the wardrobe.

Now what?

I moved toward the window and peered out to the woods surrounding the grounds on one side and the distant buildings on the other. I could go for a walk, get to know where this *Mock Hunt,* was taking place.

Voices filtered in from somewhere in the building, making me feel isolated and lonely. Maybe I could head back to the main building and find all my new friends.

I surveyed my handiwork one last time, smoothed my skirt and then touched my hair before I strode from the room. Only one chance to make a good impression and this was my moment.

I made my way out of the dorm and back along the path. Trees crowded one side of Academy lands, shadows and the scent of something...foul. I wasn't used to being this *confined*. I wanted the busy city streets and shops and shoes...God, I missed the shoes. This place felt like a damn prison.

The sound of others grew louder as I neared the main building. I shoved through the doors, and scanned the foyer. The smell of blood and flesh filled my nose. My stomach gave a twinge, but I wasn't hungry...not yet.

A sharp bark of laughter cut through the air, and I figured that was my cue. One sweep of my hair and I was heading along the hallway. The smell of fried food wafted toward me, voices droned; laughter and chatter.

Sounded like feeding time at the zoo.

Mom would be mortified.

I left the hallways behind and stepped through open double doors into the dining hall of the cafeteria. *I've arrived!* I scanned the packed tables, and all the little *cliques*; Vamps, Wolves...stilling at the asshole who ran into me earlier. He sat with his ass on the table, one foot on a chair, the other dangling while he chatted with two other furballs.

Three girls sat at the table opposite. A flash of wide, piercing eyes, and the three girls turned my way. Glorious raven black hair, perfect pale skin...I smelled feline. Such a shame.

Conversations stilled.

Heads turned...as I knew they would.

I kept my focus straight ahead, my heels clacking against the floor. They were all here, Vamps, Demons, Ghoul, all kinds of damn shifters—my gaze lingered on a girl sitting on her own, her head was down, eyes fixated on the open page of a book, hands curled into the sleeves of a sweater four times too big. She looked weird.

She lifted her head at the last minute. Her brown eyes found mine before she looked away. I strode toward the feeding troughs disguised as a buffet, cringed at the sight, and forced a smile at the poor woman standing behind the counter.

"Hungry love?" she called.

I stifled my revulsion and shook my head. "No, thank you. I ate earlier."

And then in a second, the conversations returned to normal, as though they didn't see me standing in the middle of their hall. I frowned, scanned the groups, finding the small cluster of my own kind standing in the corner of the room.

More Vamps?

I narrowed my gaze, fear mingled with aggression.

Until one of them stepped forward, out of the shadows and into the soft light. She held my gaze for a second, and then lowered her focus to the floor in an act of obedience.

At least *someone* knew who I was.

And in an instant the flare of the unknown left. I gave the dining hall one last scan, making sure there wasn't a missed opportunity for someone to rush at me and claim me as the center of attention, and then turned.

Boring.

I was already bored.

Already kinda done with it all.

Where was the fun? Where was the secret parties and kisses pressed against the lockers? Where the hell was my Dylan?

I left the dining hall behind. They never even stopped

talking, never gave me a second more than they had to. *This shit blows.*

A sign hung in the hallway...it was identical to the one I'd seen in the entrance to my dorm.

*No Magic.*

*No Killing.*

*No Fighting.*

By order of Principal Stone.

"Can this place get anymore lame?" I muttered.

Classes started tomorrow morning...I guess I was about to find out.

## CHAPTER FOUR

### HUNTING IS NEVER A SPECTATOR SPORT

"CLASS, I WANT YOU TO WELCOME OUR NEW STUDENT, Morwenna Livingstone. I'm sure she'll fit right in and I *know* you'll all make her feel welcome. I'm Ms. Amoret Lucas, I'll be taking you for Primal Studies, please take a seat and we can get started."

I winced at the sound of my name and stared at her stony expression. The teacher looked...*sweet.* Thick tortoiseshell glasses, a white cotton blouse buttoned to her neck and a thick tweed skirt that reached her knees.

That proved it...*yep, as bad as a damn convent.* Maybe it wasn't too late to ask Dad to get me out of here.

I forced a smile, straightened my spine, and a took a step. A deep snarl came from the front row. I cut a glance to the raven haired beauty from the cafeteria and caught the curl of her lip and her feline stench flare in the room.

*Jealous bitch.*

Desperation surged as I scanned for a seat and found one...right in front of the weirdo with the book. The foul scent of wet fur hit me like a slap. There he was...the walking parvovirus.

He leaned forward, arms sliding along his desk as he watched me.

He could watch all he wanted.

I cocked my hips, swishing the bottom of my skirt as I stepped toward his seat and the next, leaving Chanel No. 5 to fill the air. Let him take a whiff of how a real woman smelled.

"Pardon me." I knocked into his seat, brushing the curve of my ass against his arm. "So sorry."

And a warning snarl rumbled a little louder from the front of the class.

"That's enough," Ms. Lucas called out as I slid into my seat.

I glanced over my shoulder to the weird girl and caught her gaze. She was pretty underneath the mountain of clothes and weird hair part. But there was a sadness in her eyes, a loneliness I knew only too well.

"So, this morning is a mock hunt," Ms. Lucas called and the entire class groaned. "Come on now. I want to see what you've learned from the last time, and remember. It's not necessarily speed and strength that's important here. You need to work together as a team. Ms. Livingstone, just try to have fun and observe."

"Shit."

The mutter came from behind me. A chair scraped against the floor a second later, before the weird girl scurried around the edge of the room and disappeared through the door.

"I've got five hares out in the wooded area. They're marked from one to five...and all must be returned to me alive. I'm looking at you Judas."

There was a snigger from the guys. I turned to see

wolfboy smile and lean against the back of his chair. He seemed proud of himself from whatever happened.

"So, if you'll all make your way out to the cemetery, I'll give the signal and you can have at it."

I shifted my focus to Ms. Lucas herself. She was a little harder to read. I stared into her eyes, searching for that shine of silver, not Wolf...definitely not Vampire. Why all the animal stuff? I was a damn Vampire. The thought of a...*mock hunt,* sounded terrifying.

I didn't hunt.

I didn't even mock.

I rang a damn bell and food was delivered in a crystal glass.

Sweat broke out along the back of my neck as chairs scraped against the floor and the class rose in unison. I cut a panicked gaze to the doorway. Maybe I could hide...

"Ms. Livingstone?" The teacher called, and I cringed.

I shoved to stand and cut her a smile as I slid into step with the others and filed from the room. A tremor rippled across my chest as they all turned left. I scanned the hallway right, desperate for some place to hide and caught sight of a bathroom door. A place to hide for the duration of the hunt, and no one would notice. They'd be caught up in chasing bunnies, and me...Me, I'd stay out of sight.

One fast lunge and I left them behind, pushing the door aside and letting it close behind me. The rush of water filled the bathroom. I stepped inside, catching the weird girl standing over the basin, water dripping from the point of her chin. She froze, lifted her eyes as I neared and seized my gaze.

There was an awkward moment until she murmured. "Don't like hunts either I take it?"

That ache in my chest clenched tighter. "I don't know

how to hunt. I guess that makes me the world's worst vampire," I murmured.

I didn't even know why I told her.

She wasn't my friend. But in this moment, there was almost an alliance as she straightened and turned off the tap. "I know how to hunt, and I suck. Unlike the Wolves, and those dicks who follow Judas' every command as their alpha. He might be hot, but he's a jerk. So, I guess that makes me worse. Maybe we can scare the hares away and escape into the city." She laughed nervously.

I lifted my hand, catching the mark on the edge of my nail from cleaning my room. "I could sure do with a manicure."

She swiped the drop of water from her chin and smiled. You know, for someone who was weird, she wasn't half bad. A little makeup, tame her blonde hair and she could be quite a stunner.

"*Girls!*" The teacher's voice cracked through the air from outside. I took a hard breath, and it was mirrored by the not-so weird girl.

"I'm Mor." I reached out as she turned toward me.

She swiped a hand across her skirt and shoved it out. "Ava."

I grasped her hand in mine. Ava was a plain name, and I was sure that she had the look of a Demon, still it was nice to know someone, even if she was a little strange. I dropped her hand and motioned toward the doorway. "I guess we'd better screw this up in the most spectacular way."

There was a twitch at the corner of her lips as she nodded. I followed her out of the bathroom to where Ms. Lucas waited, arms crossed. "The hunt waits for no man...or Vampire, Ms. Livingstone, or you Ms. Blaine."

I focused on the teacher and followed the sounds of the

others all the way along the hall to the foyer. Running, sweating, biting, all the things I wasn't into. I glanced down to my ring and sighed, maybe I could find some shade and hide?

Hunting could be a spectator sport.

"I'll expect you to at least try," Ms. Lucas called out behind us. "I'll be watching...*everyone.*"

*Ugh.*

I shoved through the front doors to the academy and lifted my gaze to the hazy sun. The faint taste of blood still lingered in my mouth. Having my food delivered to my dorm was a much better option than being outside.

The others surged forward. The boys jostled and shoved each other in a macho show, seemingly to linger around the jerk I'd bumped into in the dorm. Judas. He might be hot and pleasant on the eye, but that didn't make him less of an ass. And now I knew he was the alpha of their little pack.

The girls giggled and watched, following their every move. In particular, the one with raven hair falling to her waist. She eyed Judas, admired his every move, and when he caught her watching, he winked. Yep, them two were definitely an item, and I almost choked on the cliché of the Wolf and Cat leaders dating. Maybe this Academy wasn't that much different to Beverly Hills 90210 with the jocks dating the cutest cheerleaders.

The air suddenly changed...a different kind of hunger wafted toward me like the bitter stench of cheap perfume. One I couldn't shake.

I winced as the others disappeared between the trees. Leaves crunched under my sneakers as I followed and the hazy brightness overhead faded. I followed a trail, toward the fetid stench I smelled yesterday.

A goddamn cemetery.

They expected my kind to haunt these places, when in fact...we detested them. Still, we played to the scary monster routine mortals expected for us...for the pact.

The pact was everything to the immortal races.

We learned from our past.

From the terror, from the stigma.

And now we were all about the future; cohabitation, such a dirty word. But we needed to blend in, needed to be at peace with our frail, time-sensitive companions. So, the pact was created, and it was through places like Bestias Academy where we showed mortals we were a new breed of hunters. That we had control over our supernatural sides, weren't dangerous in society, and all the stuff that made humans feel better about living amongst us.

"Okay class," Ms Lucas called behind. "We've changed things up a little this time. The hares are marked with numbers one through to five, but that's not the only thing they've been marked with. I want you to hunt based not on what you see, but on what you feel, and remember, out here...only the strong and the cunning survive."

"How is this supporting the pact?" I muttered. "I mean, I thought you didn't want us to be killers."

"That's where you're wrong Ms. Livingstone." The teacher strode closer, and then passed, cutting me a glare. "We want you to be better killers. To know your target and have better control over your instincts. What we don't want is for you to go out there in the world and just kill blindly and wantonly because you were never taught the skill of self-control."

I ground my jaw, muscles flaring as I lowered my gaze to the ugly ass skirt she wore. I'd teach her a little about self-control. I dressed to perfection, smiled and laughed on cue. I was the epitome of self-goddamn-control.

She had no idea who she was dealing with.

And all of a sudden, I understood that change in the air, that feral, primal scent that only grew stronger around me, and it wasn't cheap perfume.

It was strength. It was determination.

It was the kind of hunger that danced with desire.

The desire to win.

*The desire be the alpha.*

Goosebumps danced across my skin. Pain flared, sharp in my mouth. I lifted my hand, finger probing my gums to find the thick fang. A jolt of energy tore through me like lightning. Ms. Lucas pushed through the rusted wrought iron gates to where pale headstones covered the grounds.

But I no longer saw them.

I no longer smelled the old and gone.

I smelled the heady scent of Wolf, and Vampire, and under that I smelled *food*.

"Remember, what you see isn't always what you need to react to. Good luck class."

The bitchy girls giggled and pushed each other. My senses were heightened, drawing in their scent. Dark eyes found mine as the leader of this feline pack turned her head toward me, a flash of her animal in her eyes as she held human form...*Jaguar, fast, strong, a good climber.* And the other one by her side, gold shone in her eyes, thick, powerful thighs, strong jaw...*Lioness.* I'd need to watch out for that one. But it was the cautious glance of the last girl which sent my senses on fire. Long and lean, she was built for running. She was built for the chase, and when she looked at me with her animal eyes, a light smattering of black spots akin to a cat's fur around the corners of her eyes. *Cheetah.*

Her muscles were soft and relaxed, everything about her was calm, like she could be taking a stroll on a lazy Sunday evening. She looked almost *bored*. But deep inside my senses were firing. *Careful now.*

I dropped my hand from my mouth as the boys eased back on their haunches, a deep snarl echoing from the alpha—Judas. But as I watched him, he turned into someone else, someone with a cheeky smile and gorgeous brown hair.

And I was thrust into Beverly Hill 90210 once more. Only this was no re-run. This was real...this was happening. I cut Ava next to me a glance and saw her visibly shaken. Her skin grew pale, she looked like she might lose her lunch. Best not stand too close.

I took a slow slide away from her and caught the rise of Ms. Lucas' hand. "Good luck students...may the best hunter win."

And with the drop of her hand, a howl tore through Judas, and the rest of the pack followed. But the girls were already gone, each one tearing off into different directions, leaving the boys behind, eating their dust.

"Come on." I turned and grabbed Ava. "You're hunting with me."

"But...*but I don't...*" she spluttered.

I wrenched her close, lips curling to expose my fangs. "Today *you do.*" And we lunged in the direction of the cheetah. My breaths came hard and fast, not for survival, but for the scent. I dragged in the air, catching the faint scent of flesh and fur...and something else. *Blood.*

A deep rumble filled my ears. I turned, catching the panicked gaze of Ava as she just looked at me.

"What the fuck," she murmured.

But I wasn't listening, not to her anyway. I was listening

to that screaming inside my head. That hidden voice I'd ignored my entire life. I couldn't ignore it now.

I raced after that heady feline scent and caught a dark blur plunge through the trees at my right. The wolves were hunting, but they may as well be a herd of elephants, crashing and laughing. This was funny for them...but not for the girls.

To them this was *competition*.

Ava stumbled and fell, slipping on sodden leaves before I caught her fall. There was a flash of brown, fast, darting through the trees and the scent of something dangerous followed. Something ancient...

"I can't do this." Ava tore her sweater from my arm. "I said *I can't do this!*"

Darkness came for me, in a flash of white teeth and black hair. I shoved Ava, using everything I had and turned as the Jaguar hit me hard.

I took the brunt, flying backwards through the air before that hunger inside me took control, catching the fall before I landed on my feet. Hair flew into my eyes, blurring the feline. I brushed hair from my head.

"Watch it, *bitch*," she snarled tossing her long hair over her shoulders.

There was an edge of rage in her eyes. She didn't want me here, didn't want me anywhere near her precious class, or her boyfriend.

And with a cruel smirk she turned.

"What the hell was that?" Ava gasped and shoved from the ground, flicking away stuck leaves against her ass. "You just don't get it do you?"

I turned to her. "Get what?"

"I can't do this." She threw her hands into the air. "I'm not made for any of this...I'm not made for *anything!*"

Hysteria crowded her tone. I shook my head as she gave a brutal groan and turned and walked away. "I thought you might be different. Thought you might be...*Oh hell, I dunno what I was thinking.*"

And she just left.

Left me alone in the damn woods and confusion.

A flash of brown cut to my left, low against the ground, and it was that ancient power that called to me. I knew danger when I sensed it. Knew it in the cutting glance of my parents. I knew in the ancients, the most powerful of all of us. And it was this I narrowed in on. I shoved forward, leaving Ava behind.

The flash of brown jumped and panicked. I could hear the tiny erratic beat of the hare's heart. A flash of white against its fur 4. It was number 4. But that was the one I wanted.

A sudden snarl came from my left. The Lioness was a locomotive, head down, golden eyes blazing as her yellow hair streamed out behind her.

But it wasn't the hare she was charging at...

*It was me.*

I leapt as she reached out, swiping the air with savage claws.

"You're gonna wish you never came here," she growled.

She was strong, thundering steps punching the ground, but she wasn't agile. I lunged out of her grasp, turning on a dime to scan the trees. "What the fuck do you want from me?"

"Leave Bestias." She slowed, heaving, rasping breaths filled the air. "And never come back."

Anger burned inside me. I sucked in a breath, moving as she moved, trying to flank my side. "Not going to happen," I answered. "You just made yourself an enemy."

She smiled, and that sight made my stomach clench.

She may have made herself an enemy.

But I'd just made three.

She straightened, and then turned. "One way or another we always get what we want."

I shook my head, and watched her. Hell, I watched everything now. The snap of a twig made me jump. I scanned the trees, and then searched for number 4 hare.

He was gone...just like the one goddamn chance I had at having a normal life.

I'd left behind a life of backstabbing bitches for a pack of front stabbing bitches. "Well *shit.*"

I turned and made for the thick copse of trees that ran along an embankment and caught the *snap* of a twig behind me.

Something made me clench my fist and turn. They wanted me weak, wanted me scrambling. I shook my head. That wasn't me, not the real me. Not the one deep inside. I shoved forward, searching for that blur of movement.

*There...*

I whipped my gaze toward the movement and shook my head. If I had sleeves, I'd roll them up...and right now I really wanted goddamn sleeves. I charged forward, keeping my steps light. I left *nothing* behind. Not a scent. Not a sound. Adrenaline roared through my veins. My jaw ached, fangs desperate for release. If this what it meant to be a hunter like my father, then maybe it wasn't so bad after all.

*In this moment I was the apex fucking predator.*

I lowered my head, focusing on that movement as it came around the towering brush, and with one sudden shove I lunged through the air and hit the blur from the side.

We went down in a tumble, arms and legs flying everywhere.

The lunge might've been a ten, but the fall was definitely a one. There was a rush of warmth breath and an *oof,* underneath me. An elbow jabbed in my side. Something clonked me on the head. "Ow...*oww!*" I roared as we came to a sudden stop at the bottom of the embankment.

I lifted my head, catching the silver shine against deep brown eyes and then perfect crimson lips.

"You?" he snarled, grabbing my waist. There was a flash of hatred, the same one I saw before when we slammed into each other.

"*Y-you!*" I stuttered.

And in my head, all I could hear was my father's rage. All the centuries hating them...fighting them. "You just stay away from me."

His eyes widened, there was a flinch of surprise. "Wait," he muttered and shook his head. "Yesterday you...you took me by surprise. I didn't mean..."

I shook my head at the sudden turn around.

Didn't he know?

*We were mortal enemies.*

"I'm Judas," he muttered, rubbing his chest, and winced. There was a leaf stuck to his cheek, covering half his eye. A leaf over those grey-green eyes. My fingers trembled, desperation raged, my breaths sawing through my chest. God, he looked gorgeous.

"I don't care!" I threw my hands into the air and lifted my gaze to the steep descent.

"You came out of nowhere." He shoved against the ground and pushed to stand. "I didn't even know you were there."

"Yeah well, the whole fucking campus knew where you

were, thundering through the damn trees like a rhino in heat."

"In heat?" He snatched the leaf from his eye. There was a twitch of his lips. "Now...that's one thing I've never been called."

"Yeah, well..." Words escaped me. Heat raced, filling me with the need to take a step closer, to draw in his scent...to touch his skin. I swallowed that urge and instead took a step away. "Get used to it."

"We have our winners!" The faint voice of Ms. Lucas reached me. "Come on in class."

I ground my jaw, took one last look at my rhino and made for the steep way out of here.

# CHAPTER FIVE

## THY MUST NOT KILL

Ms. Lucas gripped her hips and stood tall near the entrance to the classroom, eyeing each of us. She wasn't impressed with our hunting skills, that was easy to see.

But from her clothes, to the delicate way she stood and even her soft voice, it surprised me she taught Primal Studies and hunting.

I'd expected something fluffier from her, like weaving... Hell, there better not be weaving in my schedule. Last time I tried to sew a button on my shirt, I almost attached the damn thing to my thumb.

The mass of students filed back into a classroom drenched in sunlight, and I dragged my feet behind the group who laughed and bumped into each other on purpose. The dull throb in the back of my head poked poisoned fingers into my temples.

I fidgeted with the ring on my middle finger. I needed to get out of this sun, get in doors where the dark would save me.

The coppery smell of blood teased my nostrils. Fresh, so

sweet and ripe. And even without seeing the body, I knew it belonged to a rabbit.

Ms. Lucas clapped loudly. "Quick. By the little show out there, we have a lot of work to do." She eyed me suspiciously as I passed her.

Did she expect me to be a top vampire hunter? My father was renowned for his stealth as much as his brutality, obviously none of those skills flowed onto me.

Everyone slid into their seats while I headed for the only remaining chair, right in the glare of the pouring sunlight. *Great.*

All eyes were on me, hatred jabbed into my back. Three felines watched my every step, their mouths twisted into silent snarls at their enemy.

Me.

The new student in class.

Hating me for hell-knows what reason.

Fuck them and their claw diggers gang.

I turned my gaze to the Werewolf. I bet the catty gang's hatred had nothing to do with the fact I was a Vampire...and everything to do with him.

On cue the hacked up furball turned his head. Silver glinted in the shine of the sunlight, and all of a sudden, I didn't notice the throbbing in my temples.

I didn't notice anything at all.

His lips curled. The smile made that dead thing in my chest shudder with promise.

*No*...my lips moved with the word. His brow raised as he searched my face. *Stay away from me.*

I swore the silver in his eyes glinted harder with the challenge.

I tore my gaze to the front of the class where Ms. Lucas was speaking.

But my gaze slipped to him once more...just like it was gravity. No, not a Wolf...I tried to clench my fist, desperately searching for that hate I needed.

Dad would be enraged.

He'd be furious.

He'd raze this school to the ground if he knew a Wolf was making eyes at his daughter.

The idea made that fossil in my chest give a slow...hard...*throb*.

A healed gash blushed along the side of his jawline and neck. Had I done that when I slammed into him, taking us both down a hill?

"This is why Vamps shouldn't be allowed in our school." The black-haired girl glared my way, her eyes flashing yellow. "No one wants you near us, zombie," she spat with poison in her words.

I slouched in my seat, holding her stare because right now I was so close to exploding and if she wanted a fight, I'd be game. But it wouldn't be fair for me, and I'd come out on the bottom of the pile.

"Enough, Ms. Lecho!" the teacher warned, and the class fell silent. "Now, who can tell me the number one rule of hunting?"

Hands shot up, but I couldn't focus on the lesson, not when I fumed, and a silent trigger inside me screamed to get up and run. Get Chuck to arrange a lift home and leave this place. I didn't want to play these games, hating how I'd somehow ended on the wrong end of everything.

But when I got home, then what?

Marry that demon knob? Hell waited for me at every turn, and knowing Thorin, he'd probably take me to meet Satan himself for our honeymoon, thinking it was romantic. Nothing that involved sweating like a beast was romantic.

I scanned the room and found Ava two seats away in the back row, hunched over her table, head low. Trying to curl herself into oblivion.

An ache flared through me as I remembered the hunt. She'd pleaded with me to leave, but I didn't listen. Yep, no wonder I never made friends.

The lights in the room switched off, plunging the room into darkness as the blinds started to descend. I glanced over to find Ms. Lucas with a remote control in hand and a white screen dropping down from the ceiling behind her desk.

I sank into the bliss as Ms. Lucas started to talk once more.

"We're going to watch how apex predators hunt in the wild, and your homework tonight is to write a five page essay on how another predator, and not your own, stalks and attacks their prey. I want you to focus on those skills they've honed, and what it means to us as we live with the pact."

Most groaned in the room, the cat girls whined and snarled. I leaned backwards, stretching my hand toward the bookshelf against the back wall behind me. I snatched the first book I touched. In haste, I set the text in my lap and ripped the corner of a page in slow motion, before returning the book titled, The Sex of Plants. Why the hell would we ever need to know that? I ought to rip out more pages, but didn't, and quickly turned around to find no one saw me. Scrunching the paper in my hand, I waited for the teacher to turn around. And the moment she did, I flung the ball in my hand toward Ava to grab her attention.

But in that exact moment, she leaned down to scratch her leg or something, and the projectile flew over her and whacked Judas in the back of the head.

*Oh, crap,* I curled forward.

He snapped around with a snarl on his lips, followed by the panther girl who'd been ogling him. She had a crease down the center of her brow. Hatred spewed from her eyes and fixed on me, and the torn pages of the open book in my hand.

Judas' two wolf friends just watched our staring match, a deep snarl rolling in their throats. When one broke into a soft howl, Judas just smirked.

Panther girl mouthed something my way.

Pretty sure it was, *you're dead.*

I jerked my gaze to the front of the class once more, yet my knees bounced in fear.

I was fucking this up on a monumental level.

The teacher cleared her throat, trying her best to draw everyone's attention. Still they stared at me. I felt them all...including Ava.

I gave her a tiny wave, offering her a smile. But she gave me the death stare and wrenched her head around so fast, she'd have whiplash.

Yep, she was pissed at me for my stunt in the woods. Bitch face loathed me. And fur ball must have thought I was interested.

I exhaled loudly and sunk deeper into my chair, hugging myself, trying to hide in the shadows of the room. I focused on the screen where a lion chased down a gazelle. When he pounced on the poor animal, the whole class cheered, clapping and hooting.

Not me. Because if this room was the Savannah, everyone else would be the damn lion and I was the gazelle biding my time until my inevitable death.

Guilt ate at me for not helping Ava when she'd opened

up to me in the bathroom. So, only one thing to do. Show her I wasn't a jerk like the rest of them at this school.

By the time class finished, hunger for the hunt echoed in every gaze. Most of the shifters were pumped, pushing and jostling against the desks before they spilled out into the hall.

Ava was fast out of her seat.

I scrambled after her, grabbing the book on predatory tactics, and tucked the goliath text book under my arm before I raced after her. "Ava, wait up!"

She slipped between the masses of students, each rushing to their next class, chatting with friends.

Shoving and pushing.

The air smelled of perspiration, fur, and freshly turned soil.

I lost her.

I pressed my back to the wall and pulled out the schedule from my school uniform's pocket, figuring I'd need a bag for my books and crap.

Rites and Rituals. Okay, didn't sound too bad. I followed the map on the back of the schedule, kept my head low and pushed through the crowd.

The hallways spilled out into classrooms. I scanned the map, stopping at a gymnasium, except there were no basketball hoops in here, no sweaty jocks and pom-pom laden cheerleaders. A group of fifteen or so students sat in a circle in the center. I hurried over, clutching my book to my chest, scanning the faces, and when they landed on bitch face, fur ball, and their clans, my stomach sank. No sign of Ava. Where the hell was she?

It meant I was alone.

I met the teacher's gaze, a tall guy with tanned skin, long dark hair curled into dreadlocks falling to his chest. He wore a purple cape with black pants and button up shirt. A black beaded chain swung as he moved, clutched onto a wooden cane.

He *felt* young...but who was I to know.

No one shifted to allow me to enter the circle. So, he waved me over, then poked one of the Judas' wolf boys to move. I squeezed in, sitting with crossed legs and my book behind me.

"I'm professor Randall Gomez your Rites and Rituals teacher." He walked within our circle holding what looked like a shoe box, and stopped in front of a girl with red curls. "Close your eyes and put your hand inside. Pick up the stone that you feel a connection with."

She followed his instructions, her hand rummaging in the box, and she pulled out a violet crystal the size of my index finger.

"Lovely," Mr Gomez said. "The amethyst is known for its anxiety properties. Hold onto your stone somewhere close because what you select is what your inner power needs you to work on."

He moved around the circle, everyone curious about others selection and what it revealed about them. When it was Judas' turn, he put his hand in and pulled out a stone instantly as if he'd known already where to select from.

"Labradorite," Mr. Gomez called out, his voice darkening. "This stone shines a light in the darkness and is used for removing hexes."

We all fell silent as Judas studied the short wand shaped crystal in his hand. It was the color of a dark opal, but what would he need warding from?

"I'm so excited." Bitch face giggled. Clearly too much attention had been on someone else for too long.

Mr Gomez lowered the box in front. "Your turn, Nesrin."

So, she had a name after all. When she pulled out a red round stone, her friends cheered, clapped while I rolled my eyes.

"Garnet," the teacher said. "This is strongly associated to magic. And *you know* that's illegal at this Academy."

Nesrin offered him her best puppy dog eyes, a hand to her chest. "I'd never."

I gagged a little at her sincerity and then stilled when he stopped in front of me.

Dark, solemn eyes found mine before he gave a small nod. "Just put your hand in...that's the way."

Fingers skimmed the inside until I touched the smooth, cold surfaces of all the crystals.

"God, she's taking forever," someone whispered.

A crystal vibrated under my touch, just slightly, sending tremors through my fingers. I grasped it, pulling it in tight against my palm before I dragged my fist free.

"Show us!" someone called out, and the teacher just nodded, and offered me a smile that said everything would be alright. But I somehow doubted that.

I uncurled my fingers to the square shaped form. Light spilled from the edges, half red like a ruby, and the other side a perfect pale green.

Someone else snorted, while Mr Gomez rubbed his jawline. "Been a while since anyone selected a tourmaline." He met my gaze. "Morwenna, this is a rare selection."

And someone snorted a laugh, but he continued, "*And* the most powerful stone for protection against negative energy. Keep it close at all times." A worrisome tone lined his words as if a piece of rock could really make a difference. I nodded and pocketed my pick.

"All right," he began. "Let's begin with a cleansing circle. Close your eyes and push everything out of your mind."

I followed, shoving the worry in my head away and settled into the meditation letting my muscles ease. Mr. Gomez's voice was smooth and soft, counting down the steps I followed inside my mind. My breaths stilled, senses eased, and that throbbing in my temples drifted away.

By the time class finished I was floating. I headed to the next class and then the next, in a blissful kind of trance. Nothing could touch me in this moment, no hate, no jealousy. No Demon boyfriend waiting in the wings.

Gaze after gaze, lesson after lesson until I slipped, exhausted, into the seat for the last class. A class filled with lessons of the pact, and how not to kill humans. I almost whimpered with relief when the bell finally rang. I shoved up from my seat, following the others. My arms were laden with books. I fumbled, stacking one on top of the other, and rushed out of the room.

Away from the prying eyes.

The whispers.

The hatred.

I hurried past Judas who leaned against the wall. He just watched me, deep brown eyes focused on my every move.

The fur ball was hot, tousled dark hair, grey-green eyes the color of a stormy sea, jawline hard like it was set in granite.

Panic filled me. I fumbled with the books, poked my tongue out at him and high tailed it out of there.

*Nice one...*I wanted to sink into a hole. Heat flooding my cheeks.

He knew he'd affected me now. *Goddamnit.* Who the hell sticks out their tongues these days? *Ugh.*

The heat burned me up from the inside out, I pushed past the doors and ran toward my dorm. The books tight in my grasp, I didn't stop until I reached my room.

And sank into the darkness.

The heavy books gave a *thud* as I dropped everything on the table, and then flopped onto the bed. I dug into my pocket, digging out my phone. Desperation welled inside me. It was so hard here, *too hard.*

*Mor:* How's your day?

I waited, tapping the screen for him to respond. When he didn't, I sent half a dozen more.

*Mor:* What are you having for dinner, A, or O?

*Mor:* Have anything planned for this afternoon?

*PAY ATTENTION TO ME!* I wanted to scream

*Chuck:* Are you in danger?

*Mor:* No.

*Chuck:* Then you know where I am if you are.

Gah. I checked my emails. Two from Dad about behaving, and three from Thorin. My fingers hovered on the *open* button. I could open them, and reply. One sentence was all I needed....

*Thorin, there's a wolf at my school...and I think he likes me.*

I thought of the fallout. There'd be terror...there'd be no more school.

No more of anything really. I'd be whisked back home in an instant, where they could control my every move. An unseen fist wrapped around my throat...choking...just like my life. Instead I tossed the phone across the bed and snatched a pillow, curling myself around it as a heaviness sat in my gut.

Leaving was prohibited, not that there was anything nearby anyway. No place to get my nails done, or visit a cafe, or try on new clothes.

Right now, it felt like as much of a prison as my own home. I looked around the room at the dull walls, bereft of furniture, well except the two beds, a desk and chair. What I needed was to decorate the place. Grabbing my phone, I clicked on my photos of my parents. I longed to be with them. To hear them ordering me around. I never thought I'd say this, but I missed their nagging.

I dragged myself out of bed. I couldn't sit here moping. I had that homework to write and a class schedule to keep up with. I sighed, and figured who better to help me with my assignment than Chuck.

One glance at my phone reminded me that he didn't want company.

Instead, I lay back against the pillow as grey-green eyes filled my head. The deep, musky scent of fur filled me, and slowly panic melted into desire. I saw him standing against the backdrop of his pack...the four of them more of a menace...a powerful determined menace.

"This is *not* happening," I snarled and rolled over, shoving my face into the pillow.

Something clattered outside my room as though a tray had fallen to the ground. I jolted upright, senses on fire and glanced to my phone. One grasp of the cell and press of the button showed it was midnight.

Must've fallen asleep.

I craned my head, listening for another sound, but none came. But I was awake now. With a sigh I pushed my feet out from under the overturned sheet, and headed to the door.

One turn of the lock and the door cracked open. Dim lights spilled under closed doors.

I stepped out and shut the door behind me before padding across the room to the balcony.

A cool breeze brushed over my thighs, and I hugged myself, rubbing my arms. An empty lawn lay below and not far in the distance were the woods, black as a raven's feather. Who knew what was in there. It gave me the chills so I headed back inside and shut the balcony door.

Crawling back in bed, I lay there, tossing and turning, my mind fully awake. But sleep refused to come. With a grunt, I climbed out of bed once more. Stepping into my ankle boots, I grabbed my leather jacket and stepped outside into the corridor while dressing myself. Great look—pajama shorts, boots and jacket.

I almost laughed at myself. I pulled the door behind me before heading down the hall, past a dozen doors. All were silent, and I took the stairs down to the lower level where there was a vending machines from snacks, to drinks, to a new machine offering small portions of refrigerated bottles of blood. Wow...And payment was a swipe of my room key.

So, I stocked up on some midnight snacks, only type A for me. An empty desk, phone and a bowl of apples sat against the wall in the foyer. Behind the desk was a map of the building.

There were more dorm buildings like this one, and a few houses marked on the outskirts of the academy compound. *Teacher's cottage,* was printed underneath each one. So, I hiked it back upstairs, cradling my four small bottles of blood.

My steps echoed, the thud slow and rhythmic as I climbed the stairs once more. I was lost in the sound as I reached the door. Until the heady scent of salty sea mixed with a metallic tang found me. I knew that scent as clear as any other. I glanced around the hallway as shivers crept up my spine. Fingers fumbled with the door handle as I turned the handle and rushed inside and then stilled.

A dark shape lay on the floor in front of me. I stuck out a hand, tapping the wall for the light switch, and blinked into the glare as the light flicked on.

A man lay on my floor.

*A mortal man.*

Lifeless.

Dead.

In his blue striped pyjamas.

His cheeks were blueish and sunken, his face stained with dried red marks.

"Fuck!" I wobbled on my feet.

Bites littered his neck, flesh torn and ripped open, blood staining his skin. The coppery smell sickened me. My stomach riled up, bile hitting the back of my throat. It shouldn't have, but it didn't smell like food to me, just like putrid death.

His brown eyes were wide, open, and dead. He wasn't even wearing shoes. God, someone had ripped him out of his bed to murder him, but why the hell was he in my room?

The bottles of blood slipped from my grasp. They bounced around my feet, the lids cracked open, and blood splashed everywhere. My legs, the wall behind me, the carpet, turning the scene into a slaughterhouse.

I stumbled away, hitting the wall with my back, my knees weakening. The smell of the sea grew stronger. I trembled and my eyes watered as I hugged myself. What the hell was going on?

Suddenly everything fell too silent.

Then an ear piercing scream rang from the doorway.

I jumped in my skin and jerked around to find Ava there.

"Holy shit he's dead...you killed a mortal."

# CHAPTER SIX

## ONE SHOULD MAKE LIFELONG RELATIONSHIPS

"I d-didn't k-kill him." I stuttered.

I shook my head, but I couldn't look away. *Dead. There's a dead body in my room.* My stomach clenched as I gagged.

The scent of blood made me hungry...but the sight of that...*that thing* made me heave.

A whimper tore from Ava's lips. Her eyes were round orbs, her breaths ragged and wheezing.

Instinct took over, my muscles flexed, and I stumbled forwards. "Please, you've got to believe me. I didn't do this. I swear to you...I swear."

Her gaze was frozen, fixed on the corpse, and I kept checking the corridor, expecting someone to come rushing out from her earlier scream. How long before someone heard us, before they came to investigate?

Sirens would blare. The hounds would come.

And of course, they'd blame the new vampire.

*The pact.*

I closed my eyes at the thought. To kill a mortal broke about fifty different laws. They'd sentence me to death, and there'd nothing Dad could do to save me.

He'd be bought before the Supernatural Council, tried like a criminal in front of the Ancients.

I was in so much trouble.

The urge to run consumed me as Ava's harsh breaths filled the space. A door slammed shut somewhere in the dorm, echoing through the hall.

I flinched and grasped Ava's arm, dragging her with me. "I promise you, I promise with everything I have, I...did...not...do...this."

She followed, cutting me a confused glare, before she stumbled toward the body.

I grasped the door and eased it closed before the lock gave a *click*.

"Fuck me!" Ava cried out, and I jerked around to find her staring down at the male. "It's Drew, the human exchange student."

Her words were a sucker punch to my gut, I lurched forward, stomach rolling...there was no more stopping my body. I darted toward my desk, grabbed the waste bin, and then retched.

"You really are the worst vampire I've ever seen," Ava muttered, while I kept choking and whimpered. "You're like those mortals who eat meat but can't stand to see where that meat actually comes from."

"Don't." I waved my hand in the air as my stomach rolled and rolled. "No more."

One swipe with the back of my hand and I rushed to my bathroom and rinsed my mouth. The cotton towel was soft and smelled faintly of lavender. I held onto that perfect scent and stepped into my room once more.

Ava prodded the body with her foot, making me whimper.

"So, you believe me?" I couldn't look away as his leg rolled with her prodding, and then fell back into place.

Ava didn't say a word.

"I'm sorry about yesterday in the woods." I was desperate. "Didn't mean to push you. Instinct took over, and I just wanted to show up those cat bitches."

And in an instant Ava turned to face me. "I won't scream. I won't even make a sound. *I will trust you,* on one condition?"

Hope surged like lightning through my chest. "What is it?"

In my head I was counting how many furs it'd take, how many houses I'd have to buy...

"You become my friend. *And not just a friend...my best friend.* We share everything, gossip, homework, stories about..." Her face grew red. "Sex. I want sex stories. I want everything. It's that or I start screaming right here...right now."

I flinched, my mind scrambling to keep up.

"We put each other first, *always.*" She placed her hands on her hips

"Wait," I muttered. "You don't want money? Power? Fame? You don't want my dad to get you the world?"

"What do I want with the world if I'm lonely?" she muttered.

I saw it all then, all the missed goddamn signals. I used her, and forced her aside in the hunt. I didn't see her as anything other than a means to an end. But that wasn't how she saw me. "You don't want to...get with me or anything, right? I mean it's cool and all...I just don't swing that way."

"I don't want to have sex with you, Morwenna. Get over yourself." Her face burned as she looked away. "I just want a friend. I want someone I can share stuff with. I want someone who gets me. I just figured we could...I dunno."

Guilt filled me. "Yes. Yes, I'll be your friend."

She jerked her gaze high, meeting mine. There was a flare of surprise, dark eyes glinting before she smiled. "Really?"

"Really," I answered and reached out my hand. "Buddy."

She glanced at my outstretched fingers and took a step forward taking my grasp in hers. "Okay...okay then, we have to do something with that," she pointed at the body. "While we try to figure out what happened."

She was cool, calm and confident, running off a list of things like she'd done this all before. Confusion filled me, but I didn't care about that right now. I'd ask a million questions later, after all, we were now apparently BFFs.

"We have to hide it," she murmured.

My stomach protested again, and nausea rocked through my head as I lifted a finger and pointed. "I'm not touching that *thing*."

Chuck filled my head. He'd worked for Dad and would know how to dispose of it. But then they'd come, take me away. They'd blame me even though none of this was my fault.

Nope, I'd take care of this myself.

Ava rolled her eyes and marched across the room. She ripped the sheet off my bed and lay it on the carpet near Drew.

God, poor sucker.

"Who do you think killed him?" I muttered watching her bend and wrap the edge of the sheet under his body before draping it over his head.

"I don't know," she grunted. "It's not like everyone's excited having you in class."

"You think it's them...those *cat bitches?*"

Ava shrugged and grabbed a towel from my bathroom before wrapping it around his wound. "Everyone here hates mortals. It's why Drew lived in the house with teachers on the compound. No idea why they'd do an exchange with a human in the first place."

She used her foot to roll Drew onto the blue sheet. Within a minute, she had him packed tight and wrapped like a mortal burrito.

I lifted a hand, covering my mouth as I heaved with the thought.

"Who the hell are you?" I asked.

She glared my way. "You going to help or just make commentary? And haven't you watched Dexter? It's the 101 guide to disposing of bodies."

"Hate shows about murder," I murmured, and Ava shook her head.

"Everyone knows who your dad is, and you hate murder?"

I wanted to respond, argue I wasn't like my parents, but I didn't have it in me when we had more pressing issues.

"Okay, what's the plan, then?" I asked instead.

"The basement. There's a ton of crap and boxes in there, so we hide him for now, get him out of here then we clean up any evidence. Then we find a way to get rid of the body for good so it can't be tied to you."

"And figure out who the hell tried to set me up." I muttered.

Ava straightened, strode to the doorway and turned the lock. She stuck her head out and then turned to me and whispered. "All clear."

She moved back to the dead burrito's head and shuffled her hands under his shoulders before she stilled and cut a glare to me. "Hello, you gonna help?"

Cringing on the inside I stepped closer. But the moment I touched his foot, I flinched. Ava grumbled, muttering something about being as weak as a damn mortal and heaved. I ground my jaw and averted my gaze as I grabbed him around the knees and slowly walked backwards out of the room.

The smell was bad, but the feel of him thumping against my thighs...all cool, and *moist*.

"Swear to god, if you vomit all over him, you're on your own."

I swallowed back the bile. It was just shoes...heavy fucking shoes. Jimmy Choo's, Nike trainers. *Just heavy as fuck shoes...*

"It's heavy. I can't get a grip." I scanned the balcony, left and right.

"Use your vampire strength," Ava hissed with sarcasm in her voice.

Using her foot, Ava pulled the door shut behind us. We shuffled quickly toward the doorway marked *stairs*.

I used the wall to slide my back along as I passed through and Ava came behind, stopping to close the door and then we were moving once more. A leg fell from the burrito wrapping and slipped from my hands. I lunged forward, sweaty palms slipped, but it hit the ground with a *thud* that rang just a little too loud.

"Shit." Ava stumbled and the body slumped, head hitting the railing with a *dong*.

"Careful." I bent and tried to stuff his foot back in.

"Me? *You* were the one who let him go," she hissed, moving past me, and picking up his feet.

*Thump...thump...thump...*She dragged him feet first down the stairs. I tried to keep up, waddling forward to grab what I could, until his hand flung upwards and grabbed my breast.

"Eww." I batted him away and fell on my ass, goose-bumps lining my arms. "He touched my boob."

Ava smothered a bark of laughter. "You're just gross."

Fine. I picked him up, avoiding that creepy hand and we moved fast. I scanned the stairs over my shoulder and kept on moving until we hit the ground floor.

Ava moved so damn fast I practically had to run to keep up with her. Where was this agility and strength during the hunting class?

Finally, she paused, and I pressed a shoulder into the wall, muscles strained and aching.

Holding Drew with one arm, she pushed open the door to the basement, and we darted inside.

I shut the door behind us with a small kick and we were thrown into darkness. "Shit! I can hardly see a thing."

"Follow my lead, I have nocturnal sight."

Stunned, I stumbled after her, and curiosity got the better of me. "I didn't know you were a cat shifter too?"

"I'm not," she snarled.

"An owl? Fox, or a racoon? They're so cute."

"Don't want to talk about it. Can we focus?"

"Oh yeah, for sure." I made a mental note to research all nocturnal animals if I survived tonight.

"Here, we hide him here," she declared. We stopped suddenly, and all I could make out around me was dark shapes in the form of boxes surrounding us.

"Where exactly is here?"

"Just follow my lead." She ripped off a lid from an oversized box. "They store wooden crates here for collection from deliveries of anything the Academy orders."

"How do you know all this?"

Ava tugged on Drew, and I followed her lead as we pushed his curled body into an oversized box. "I like to explore."

I pushed down on his foot, but it wouldn't fit. "Shit."

Something creaked from deeper in the basement.

We froze and looked up. Her breath raced, heavy on my cheek as we clutched each other.

Fear was a cinched straitjacket around me. There was a scuff of a shoe... "Did you hear that?" I whispered.

"Yes." Ava shoved Drew's in and jammed the lid back on the crate. With my hand in hers, she ran, dragging me behind her. We sprinted through the dark, shivers racing up my spine, the hair on my nape shifting.

We burst out of the basement, shut the door, and raced back to my room.

Locking the door behind us, I pressed my back to the door, gasping for air. I didn't need it, but right then, I inhaled it as if my life depended on it. Ava's face was ashen.

"Do you think someone was there with us?" I asked.

"Don't know. Maybe it was just a rat."

"Hell." I spied the empty space where Drew was minutes earlier, and the splatters of blood from the bottles I'd dropped. "We need to clean this up."

So, we broke into auto mode. I collected equipment from the cleaning cupboard, and without a word we scrubbed and cleaned until not a speck of red remained. On the bright side, the spillage should mask the smell of Drew in here. But just to be on the safe side, I took my Chanel N.5 and sprayed half of the expensive stuff onto the carpet where the body had lain.

"What do you think?" I asked.

Ava nodded her head, though her nose wrinkled from the heavy fragrance. Better smelling sweet than like a rotting corpse.

"I can't believe we just did that," I said. "Thanks for helping. I couldn't have done it on my own."

"That's what besties do for one another. I got your back."

Regardless of the creepy factor of her sudden clinginess, I appreciated having her with me. No one was perfect, right?

I went to respond, when a siren wailed through the dorm, robbing me of the sliver of hope and calm I clung to.

Ava and I exchanged glances, and my legs wobbled beneath me as she muttered. "Fuck, we're busted."

# CHAPTER SEVEN

## ONE MUST STRIVE FOR THEIR FULL POTENTIAL

An alarm rang in my ears from the overhead speaker in my room, piercing my soul.

Ava and I stared at the bucket and mop sitting against the wall, filled with bloody water. Evidence was just sitting out in the open. All we needed was for Principle Stone to march in here and catch us red handed.

*Crap.*

Voices filtered in from outside the room. Leaving me panicked and pissed off, sending shivers scattering over my flesh.

Adrenaline flooded me, and without a word, we both lunged. I clawed the bottles and mess from the floor as Ava rushed into the bathroom. The hiss of the shower followed. We were quiet as we could be, pouring the dirty, bloody water down the drain. "The bleach," I muttered and glanced over my shoulder. "Pour the rest."

We scrubbed until our knuckles were raw.

"What do we do now?" she asked straightening her spine and swiping the back of her hand across her brow.

I grabbed the bucket and mop, stuffed them into the

corner of my bathroom. "If anyone asks, I'll say I've been cleaning up my room." And Principle Stone could attest to it from our earlier conversation.

Swallowing the lump in my throat, I hurried to the front door and looked over at Ava. "Okay, we know nothing, and we're in my room because we're friends and doing a sleepover."

"We *are* friends," she repeated.

"Sure." I could only deal with one thing at a time and opened the door, pretending to yawn, ready to step outside. Ava was on my heels, but no one seemed to notice. They stumbled around like lost sheep, asking what was going on.

"*Morwenna!*" Thunder filled my room. The deep, violent snarl came from behind me.

I sighed. This was why I didn't need a babysitter.

Ava was at my side, whimpering. "Umm, there's a huge freaking vampire in your room."

I shut my door and spun to face Chuck who was stepping inside from the balcony door.

"Wow, great way to draw attention," I barked.

"Is there something I shouldn't be drawing attention to?" One bushy eyebrow arched upward. He eyed Ava suspiciously, his brow furrowing.

"Ava, this is my guard, Chuck, who isn't allowed to be in this dorm. Chuck this is my friend and next door neighbor, Ava. Okay, now you've met, what the hell are you doing here?" I glared his way.

"The alarm went off, so I came to check on you." He was motionless in black jeans and an open-collar shirt. There was no armor, no knives...anyone could almost mistake him for looking normal.

*Almost.*

The buttons of his shirt strained with every breath

against a powerful chest. He commanded the room, swallowing an entire corner. Anyone might mistake him for a statue, stony eyed and unmovable. And did the guy ever wear pajamas? If he did, I'd never seen them.

"Right. Of course. Ava and I were having a sleepover, and we were headed out to see what was going on. So strange."

He narrowed his gaze, studying me.

"We're best friends actually," Ava chipped in, fumbling over her words. "*And* we just had a pillow fight." She flipped her hair and sucked in hard breaths, pretending to look flustered.

"A pillow fight?" He muttered and eyed me suspiciously and then stared at my bed and the missing bedsheet. *Damn*, I needed to get that addressed.

"I spilled some perfume," I muttered and glared at Ava as soon as he looked to the half bottle of Chanel No. 5 on my nightstand.

"Ah, *yes*. That's what happened. You know us girls...*sooo clumsy*."

He swung his gaze back to us, first stilling on Ava until she squirmed and then settling on me. Only, I was used to the long glaring looks.

*And I didn't falter...ever.*

"We're safe, we're settled," I snarled. "Thank you for checking on us, but you better leave before someone sees you."

"Where are you staying in the Academy?" Ava was curling her finger through her blonde hair, staring at Chuck with those eyes...the doe eyed ones.

I grabbed Ava by the elbow and drew her closer to me and spoke through clenched teeth. "I'm sure he has better things to do." I forced the biggest smile before I turned and mouthed the words, *what the hell are you doing?*

There was a dead body in the basement, and I didn't need Principle Stone finding Chuck in my room as though we were cleaning up a kill.

Ava pressed in closer to me, so close her bubblegum breath wafted to my nose.

"*You* didn't tell me you had a hunk for a guard."

"Maybe you forgot your glasses. *That* is not a *hunk*. He's a damn Vampire," I snapped.

"He's hot, and when he looked at me, I think my nipples twitched."

I stilled, cold. Tried to count to three and then turned. "He's too old for you."

"So, Vamp years are like dog years right? How old is that in normal years?"

"*He* can hear everything you're saying," Chuck muttered.

Ava blushed and giggled.

"As long as you're okay." The corners of Chuck's mouth curled. "Good night, Ava. It's been a pleasure."

What the hell?

And in a second, he was gone, striding through the open door to my balcony, and launching his massive frame over the bannister and into the night.

"Did you see the way he looked at me?" Ava swooned and collapsed onto my bed.

I gagged. "Don't even go there, trust me. Now, come on, we have to go join everyone else." And with a moan of protest, she shoved against the mattress and was on her feet.

We slipped out of my room, merging with the other moaning students.

Someone rushed down the corridor, brandishing a torch

like a damn weapon as they hurried forward. A second later, glaring overhead lights came on, and I stared at a ruffled, pajama wearing Ms. Lucas.

"I want all students down in the foyer *immediately.*"

I glanced to Ava who just shrugged. We filed in line with the others, stumbling and snarling as they made their way down the stairs to find so many more students than resided in this dorm. We were all being gathered here.

Green eyes flashed my way. Nesrin and her pack of cats strode as one in front of us. I turned my head, making sure Ava was right beside me.

I wasn't alone now. Not so easy to label as prey. The thought filled me, and I wrenched my gaze back to her. *Did she do this?* Did she...set me up?

Gold eyes seized mine as the entourage turned and met my stare.

*Fucking bitches.*

"One of the young mortal exchange students has gone missing. We're going to be conducting a search of all properties on the compound and that includes your rooms. So, everyone must stay here together while we do that."

There was a groan and a snarling murmur.

A ruffled Ms. Lucas shot her hand in the air, stilling the sound. "I don't care. A mortal's life is at stake people, and *we* will do our utmost to make sure he's found alive and well."

"Do you think he's dead?" Someone called from the back of the crowd.

Ms. Lucas said nothing, just met our gaze, and then continued. "We're not interested in any contraband you might have, we are just looking for a mortal...*that's all.*"

The dorm doors opened behind her. In strode Principal Stone and about eight other teachers. The Principal glanced to Ms. Lucas and then lifted her hands. "Let's go, room by room, split up and check each dorm building."

My stomach hardened like a damn rock. Ava took one slow side-step toward me. Warm fingers reached out, grasping mine. On any other day, I might've shuddered and recoiled in fear.

But not today.

Today I grasped her hand tight...and together we held on.

The teachers were a darkened blur, racing up the stairs and then moving through every room.

Doors opened. Doors closed.

A whisper slithered across the nape of my neck. I turned, catching all three catty bitches staring at me. Nesrin lowered her gaze catching my hand grasped in Ava's and her lips curled into a sneer.

I didn't care what they thought. Didn't care at all. Ava was a damn rock, standing beside me. She could've screamed. She could've not believed me when I pleaded that I had nothing to do with this. But she didn't. She stayed. She was *my friend.*

Darkness shifted in the at the edges of my vision. I turned my gaze to the Vamp girl at the back of the crowd. Cold, unflinching eyes met mine before she turned away. I'd seen her in the cafeteria, stepping out of the shadows and leaving the few other Vampires behind. They all kept to themselves. She broke the stare, instead finding Ms. Lucas as she stepped out of a room and stopped in the middle of the landing. Two teachers followed, and one by one they made their way downstairs. We waited until other teachers arrived from the other dorms before they made an announcement.

"It's all clear," Principal Stone called. "Everyone can go back to their dorm rooms."

There was a growl and a mutter, before the Principal's head snapped toward the sound. "Classes *will* begin at the normal time in the morning, so I suggest you get settled."

"It *is* morning, Miss!" someone called.

She said nothing, just strode down the last stair and scanned each of us, stilling on me for a second before moving on. The rest of the teachers left us to stand around in the middle of the foyer.

"This is *bullshit*," someone snapped behind me. "A damn mortal breaks the academy rules and goes drinking in one of the nightclubs and we get hauled out of bed in the middle of the night."

"Probably passed out in a gutter somewhere. Mortals *cannot* hold their liquor."

"You're telling me," someone else called. "I have one for a companion back home. She's always falling asleep."

"That's cause you take too much from her vein, Sapphira," another called, and a wave of laughter broke out.

One by one they climbed the stairs, and doors opened and closed once more, leaving Ava and I standing...as well as the cats.

"You look guilty, *Vamp*," Nesrin snarled, baring her teeth.

"*You* look ugly, *Panther*," Ava answered in response. Her voice low, and unflinching.

The three cats turned their head, finding Ava's stare. I clenched my grip, loving her in this moment.

The doors squealed as they were yanked open, and in a rush three wolves filled the space. Were they staying in this dorm too? I didn't remember seeing their name on the chart near reception, unless they still hadn't left for their own dorm yet.

"Everything okay?" Judas strode forward, turned his head, and nodded to the two other wolves at his side in dismissal.

They were gone in a heartbeat, striding up the stairs, taking three or four at a time.

"Yes, *thank you,* Judas." Nesrin stepped away from the others and wrapped her arms around him. "I wasn't sure what was going on. I hope the mortal is safe."

Judas said nothing, only met my gaze over the top of her head.

Until Nesrin pulled away. She caught the connection, glancing my way to give me daggers. "I was in the most glorious sleep." She feigned a yawn and stepped backwards, until she stood in front of me. "I was dreaming about us."

"All good," one of the wolves came down the stairs.

I hadn't even seen where they went.

"Thank you, Nero, and Bond," the Panther murmured and fluttered her lashes. "We feel so much safer knowing your dorm is right next to ours."

Heat flared through my chest at the thought. *I bet they did.*

"Everything's locked." The other wolf glanced to Judas. He lifted a hand, dragging fingers through dark, mousy brown hair and glanced at me.

"I'm going to bed," the Lioness muttered and turned her back on the others. "See you guys in a few."

The Cheetah was next, glancing at Nesrin before smiling. "Me too, I'm beat."

"And then there were two," Judas glanced from Nesrin to me.

*"Three,"* Ava snapped. "Or am I just chopped fucking liver?"

He just smirked, and shook his head. But Ava tried to stifle a yawn. "Actually, I'm out too."

"Me too," I muttered and turned, leaving them in our wake.

The two other wolves watched me as I strode past and along the stairs. Ava glanced over her shoulder and then back to me, leaning in close to whisper. "What's with all the staring?"

I looked back and gave a shrug. But inside I was reeling. Did Judas come to check the dorm for Nesrin's safety...or for mine? Or did it have something to do with the missing human?

*Don't think like that. Mortal fucking enemy, remember?*

I'd warned him. I'd given him every opportunity to stay the hell away from me. Murmured voices reached my ears. Nesrin was whispering good night. I didn't turn my head, just kept my focus forward and walked Ava to her room.

Her deep brown eyes flashed as she stepped inside her room and then closed the door.

But she never did tell me why she was passing my room in the middle of the night...

I stared at her closed door, questions lingering on the tip of my tongue as a door opened and closed down at the front of the building. A dark blur raced through the foyer and then up the stairs.

"I came as fast as I could."

I flinched at the words behind me and spun catching Judas racing to the top of the stairs He glanced at Ava's closed door and then focused on me.

"I-I warned you before," I stuttered, catching movement

as the two other wolves took the last step to still beside the bannister near the stairs.

"One thing you should know about me," Judas murmured, silver glinting in his eyes. "I'm *always* up for a challenge."

I shook my head. "This is no challenge...it's a warning," I stated and glanced toward my room. "You know who my father is?"

He shook his head and stepped closer, "I know...and *I don't care.*"

He met me at the edge of the doorway to my room. That heat in my chest turned into a damn inferno. The dead muscle in my chest throbbed to life as Judas braced one hand against the wall, cutting me off.

I should be angry.

*I should be pissed.*

But that silver in his eyes seized me. My emotions were a rampage, mingling into a catastrophic tornado inside.

"You're breathing hard. I can hear you panting," he murmured.

I was transfixed by those perfect lips as his words jumbled inside my head. "What did you say? *You can smell my panties?*"

He blanched and lowered his hand.

*"What kind of sick fuck are you?"*

Nerves took me until my mind bordered on hysteria. So much had happened tonight, and keeping my thoughts and mouth in check seemed impossible apparently. But I held my head high, ignoring the heat slithering up my spine.

Doors opened once more. Others stepped out and turned to find us together.

Judas just shook his head, the corners of his lips curling into a grin. "You know." He lifted his hand, and pointed at me. "You are one crazy Vamp. AND IT'S A GOOD THING I LIKE CRAZY!" He roared at the top of his voice and laughed as he turned toward the rest of his pack.

My heart was booming, filling my head with the deafening sound. I pressed my spine against the wall, my damn knees trembling. One panicked glance behind me and I caught Ava watching through her cracked open door.

I tried to smile and slid along the wall, fumbling for my door. I didn't trust my damn knees...or that hollow pounding in my chest. I hit the handle, shoved open the door as everyone slipped into their rooms again.

"What the hell," I muttered and closed myself in my room.

The light was glaring but I didn't care. I lifted my hand and motioned into the air. "Blah," my words resounding like a goddamn crazy person in my head. "I can smell your panties? Why the fuck would I say that?"

And the only answer I received was the echo of the Wolf inside my head. *You are one crazy Vamp. And it's a good thing I like crazy!*

He liked me...

*He liked me...*

"Oh shit."

# CHAPTER EIGHT

## VAMPIRES SHALL NOT SUNBATHE

I TOSSED AND TURNED AND TURNED IN BED. ALL I could see was wide open eyes and bite marks on the body on my floor. Bite marks which covered his neck and his chest. I shifted again. *A body on my floor.* It couldn't have been a coincidence and thanks to my big goddamn mouth I had plenty of enemies.

The cat gang filled my mind. What were they hoping to achieve? Have me discredited and thrown out of the school? I'd embarrass my father, make a mockery of our entire clan.

Sleep stayed away as I scooted toward the edge of the bed.

They wouldn't win.

I'd figure this out and trace it back to them.

I may be shit at the biting and the killing, but I knew how to get down and dirty, cat gang style. Ava would help me, together we'd find the evidence we needed and then we'd go to Principal Stone. We'd figure this out...and then that just left the Wolves.

I flopped back to the bed, and closed my eyes. Sleep came for me fast, despite my whirling thoughts.

Until what felt like minutes later the chirp of my phone shattered my peaceful slumber. I cracked open my eyes, finding brown eyes staring back at me.

*"Jesus!"* I roared and slammed backwards so fast my head hit the wall.

Ava knelt next to my bed, her toothbrush stuck out from between her lips. "So," she muttered, and all I saw was white toothpaste on her lips. "You and Judas."

I blinked hard, trying to process her words. "You heard us?"

She shrugged. "Maybe."

I eyed her, trying to decipher if she was fishing for information or had honestly been privy to the mortifying words I'd said last night. And if she'd heard them, hell... how many others in the nearby rooms did as well?

"So, which is it?" I grabbed her arm, needing to know or I might never be able to show my face in public again. I'd crawl back under my covers and stay hidden for eternity.

"God, your touch is like ice." She shook me off and retreated to the hallway, still brushing her teeth.

"Yeah well, I haven't eaten yet." I scrambled after her, tracking her into her room, then paused in her doorway, my attention caught on the array of beach shells of every size and color plastered to the walls. "Why does it feel like Atlantis in here?"

"Reminds me of home, and most were gifts from family," she called out from the bathroom. The sound of running water shut off, and she joined me in the main room, wiping her mouth with the back of her hand. "Anyway." She pressed her back to the wall, seductively, staring at me with a teasing gaze. "Tell me more about you and Judas."

Someone strolled past the door out in the hall, and I hurried to shut us inside. "I'm so embarrassed," I admitted, turning to Ava. "I asked Judas if he could smell my panties." And just saying the words had me burning up. I dropped my face into my hands, cringing at the words. "Then he said I was crazy and he admitted to liking crazy," I murmured.

Ava seized my wrists and pulled my hands from my face. "Shit, you said that?"

Ignoring the shock of her face, I exhaled a breath of relief. She hadn't heard, so neither did anyone else. Well except Judas and most likely his two wolves. And I could live with that. I'd ignore them, stay away and not melt in a puddle of humiliation.

"He likes you, hey?"

Perhaps I misunderstood him, misheard his sarcasm when he said he liked crazy.

"Don't think he meant it like that." Because I didn't need that kind of complication in my life, to be involved with Dad's mortal enemies in any way, to get Dearest Daddy hyped up and threatening my peers.

Ava raised a perfectly sculptured eyebrow as her gaze scanned over me. She slouched on one leg, arms folded across her white school blouse with the academy emblem above her heart. A wolf's head, mid-howl, encased by a simple black circle.

"That's not how it sounded to me."

My mouth dropped open. "You did hear us!"

She giggled. "Hell yeah. I had my ear to the door once I heard voices in the hall."

My knees softened a bit, just enough to remind me others could have done the same from their rooms, and now a fiery furnace climbed up my neck and over my cheeks.

Ava patted my arm. "I'm sure no one will remember it, plus we've all done worse things."

I turned after her, somehow not believing I'd ever

forget. "What worse things have you done?" Misery loved company, right?

She opened the door to the hallway. "You gonna change out of your pajamas?"

Looking down, I completely forgot I hadn't even showered, so I hurried back into my room to get ready, needing to push aside the embarrassment. And I made a decision to stay low, not draw attention to myself. Focus on finding out who killed that human and dumped his body in my room. Watch the cat gang's every move until they slipped up. Everyone slipped sooner or later and I'd be there to see it.

The rest of the day flew past in a blur of classes, mock-fighting training, and even a cooking class using only ingredients from the woods thrown into the mix. Every lesson came down to survival, raw, primal instincts to live off the land without human intervention. To protect ourselves. Maybe I'd been guarded by Dad for too long because everyone else seemed to excel, including Ava.

Except me.

The protected Vampire.

At every opportunity, I stayed as far from the wolves and cats as I could, and they left me alone. Win, in my books.

After a long day, my mind refusing to calm, sleep didn't come that night. I climbed out of bed, tired of stirring. Tired of worrying. Tired of not knowing who'd set me up. I had to do something, anything to stop the panic spinning my thoughts into tangled knots.

Stumbling about in my room in the dark, I got changed into jeans, hoodie, and my boots. Perfect stalking outfit. Once out in the hall, I moved with silent steps to Ava's door, my stomach somersaulting about asking her to join me. For purely selfish reasons of course; I didn't want to go alone. Plus, we were now cohorts in this whole *dead-body-in-my-apartment* fiasco.

I raised my hand and gently knocked... so soft there'd be no way she heard me, so I reached down to the handle on the off chance she hadn't locked the door.

The door swung open, and I flinched backward, a tiny gasp falling from my lips.

Ava stood in the doorway gripping a baseball bat, raised over her shoulder. She frowned upon seeing me, her earlier war-like expression melting away.

"Whoa," I said. "Relax, it's just me."

"Holy cow, Mor, you scared the hell out of me." She seized my wrist, glanced left and right in the hall, then heaved me into her room. She shut the door with a small click.

"Couldn't sleep either?" I eyed her dressed in jeans and tee. "Nice weapon."

She marched toward her bed and tucked the bat underneath. "You never know when you'll need it. There's a murderer on campus." She turned toward me. "Plus, my ex got it for me and it's the only thing I have left of him."

"What happened between you two?" I reached out for her, but she looked away.

The silvery moonlight beamed into her room and illuminated her blonde locks, bringing attention to the pain on her face. "Don't wanna talk about that. I prefer to know why the heck you were outside my door, freaking me out."

I slouched, stuffing my hands into the pockets of my jeans. "I can't stop thinking about Drew," I murmured. "Need to find out who did this before they return for me."

"Then let's go." Showing no hesitation, Ava stepped

into her sneakers, and warmth spread through my chest. So, this was what having a friend felt like? Being able to rely on someone who always had my back? I loved it in truth and wished I'd found more close friends years ago.

"What's the plan?" she continued.

"Go check out his dorm and find clues. Do you know where he stayed?"

Ava's eyebrows raised. "Is that all I am to you? Invaluable information?"

"No, it's—"

She chuckled lightly and stretched her back. "Only kidding. Now, should I bring my bat? We could say we're playing midnight baseball? That's something Vamps do, right?"

"Ha ha. This isn't Twilight." I turned to the door and opened it a smidgen. When I was convinced no one was out there, we snuck out.

"What about you turning into an animal? Can you do that like Dracula does in movies?" she queried, a smile in her voice.

I cut her a stare, filled with daggers. "I'm a real Vamp not a made up one. We don't turn into bats or mist or any of that other shit. We drink blood and are allergic to the sun. Simple."

"You make it sound like a disease."

I didn't respond. Couldn't, because I'd often wondered if being born a Vampire was a curse. We had so many limitations. Constantly needing to feed to keep our hunger in check, no sunlight, and everyone seemed to hate us for some reason. Sure, being part of a mob Vampire family didn't help, but I'd never hurt a soul. Our blood at home was ordered from donors, and it was organic.

With Ava on my heels, we hurried in silence down the

stairs and crept outside the dorm. A cold breeze wrapped around me, tossing my long hair across my back. Something about the night heightened my senses. The sharpness of the shadows, the tiny sounds of critters nearby, the peacefulness of the moon shining in the tapestry overhead.

"Which way?" I glanced over to the left, the same path that lead to Chuck's shack, and coldness curled in the pit of my gut. What if he stalked the grounds and saw us? "We need to move and fast."

"This way." Ava swung right toward the brick two-story building where everyone ate meals most days. Beyond that, we ran side by side in the dark. I had no idea where we were going, but I followed Ava's lead, trusted her.

She cut me a strange look.

"What?"

"Your hair shines in the moonlight, did you know that?"

"It does?" I ran my fingers through the dark strands and lifted the ends in front of my face. Hell, she was right. My hair had a highly luminous sheen. Why hadn't anyone told me about this before? Maybe because Dad kept me indoors and I hardly interacted with others. Those who worked at the mansion would never step a foot wrong in fear of Dad's wrath. I pulled my hair into a ponytail and tucked it under my hood, then pulled that over my head, just in case it revealed us in the dark.

"I think it's pretty." Ava stopped near a cottage, running her hands through hair blonde hair.

"Yours is pretty too." Was that what I was supposed to say?

When she smiled, I guessed I was right, but we didn't have time to exchange compliments. Not now when someone could find us, when Chuck could be stalking the grounds and uncover us sleuthing.

"This is one of the teacher's dorms and where Drew lived while at the Academy."

The cottage hunkered low in the darkness, shadows from lofty trees nearby making it look more like an oversized wolf, curled up and fast asleep. It had stone walls with a thatched roof and could easily belong in a fairy tale.

I leaned closer to Ava, both of us shrouded in the shadows. "If no one heard him leave, whoever kidnapped him did it through his bedroom window." I'd watched my fair share of murder mysteries and 99% of the time, the most plausible answer was the correct one.

"Good place to start."

We started to circle the house, creeping under the windows. The first one was covered in curtains and seeing inside was impossible. Studying the dusty ground showed no footprints or anything, so we moved on to the next one and the next. Coming back around to the front after doing a complete loop of the property, I sighed. One window to go. Ava and I exchanged hopeful glances.

On tippy toes, I peered inside from the corner of a window with no curtains. The moonlight revealed a basic living room with an L-shaped lounge in front of an unlit fireplace. No television. Who were these people? Barbarians?

"Ohh." Ava voice squeaked, like she found evidence.

I ducked and spun away from the house to find her crouched a few steps away, her back to me.

"What did you discover?" I rushed over to see her holding a handful of grass.

"What is that?" I muttered, studying the plants for blood droplets or something.

"I just found a four-leaf clover."

Staring at her, gobsmacked, I was close to ripping them

out of her hand. "Pretty sure that's not going to help us find Drew's killer," I snapped, then glanced around us. My skin rippled as the breeze whistled past, the trees rustling, and somewhere in the distance, an owl hooted. Anyone that looked out their window could see us.

Ignoring me, she plucked out the grassy strands in her fist, left holding only the four-leaf clover. "This is a sign. Mom always told me to collect any luck I found as it would scare away evil."

"Okay, let's agree to disagree." My family were as superstitious as they came. Like they believed if a human broke a mirror and uttered a real vampire's name, they could invoke our final death. I'd yet to see an inch of proof that any of that stuff was real in any capacity.

"There's nothing here. We need to go." I nudged at her elbow to get her moving when she gasped so loudly that the entire campus probably heard her.

I flinched, bumping against her, my gaze swinging right and left seeing nothing but night. Yet my stomach pressed the back of my throat. "What is it?"

She was pointing to something near a tree, and when I followed her line of sight, I spotted it. A dark paw print at the base of the tree.

"Holy shit. Is that a werewolf print?"

We scrambled closer and fell to our knees nearby. The mark had blood on it and faced away from the tree. I glanced up and spotted an enormous branch hanging over the roof of the cottage, directly over a large chimney.

"They used the chimney," I stated. "I have no idea how, but they must have dragged him out that way."

"Magic? Santa Claus?"

"It's illegal. And you know Santa's real and a Vamp, and he eats kids?"

She glared at me, holding back the smile on her lips. "Do you always destroy people's dreams?"

Ava climbed to her feet, and I joined her. She wriggled the four-leaf-clover in my face, smirking.

"Fine, the stupid plant was a sign."

When one of the lights in the cottage switched on, I shuddered.

Without hesitation, we darted into the shadows without pause.

"Do you think it's Judas and his wolves?" she asked.

"I don't know." But we ran, and something in my chest ached. Sure, Judas was a class-A ass, but was he a murderer?

When we reached our dorm, we split and went to our own rooms in case anyone followed us.

I ripped off my clothes and jumped into my pajamas before leaping into bed. And I lay there, heaving for breath.

The paw print.

It had been a damn Wolf.

The image revolved in my mind, along with the possibility that Judas might be involved. I couldn't remember how long I stirred in bed, but before I closed my eyes, silver eyes glinted in my mind.

*Goddamn Wolves*...the thought started and there it ended.

Darkness swept in, stealing the thought...stealing everything.

The rest of the week passed by in a blur, and nothing happened at all. No one came to hunt down Ava or I after our snooping. No one found the body down in the basement either, but we couldn't leave it there much longer as it would start smelling. But it would have to wait a while longer.

The cops were on campus, working on the case of the

missing boy. Another reason Ava and I kept our heads low and watched everything from the shadows.

We went to class, ate on our own in the cafeteria, and returned to our rooms. We'd spent so much time together this past week, it felt like we'd been friends for years.

Now, it was Saturday morning and I tapped the keyboard loudly, frantically needing to finish an assignment on why giants went extinct. Who the hell gave a shit, anyway? And why did we need to attend class and submit homework on the weekend? After ten minutes of researching online, I went with the theory that if megalodons were extinct from a lack of prey and increased competition from predators, then so could giants. How much would a giant need to consume in a day to stay sated? At least a village's worth of people. Of course, no one knows the real reason, so technically no one's argument was wrong, but the megalodons theory seemed most logical to me.

"They're interviewing everyone," Ava cried out, bursting into my room, her cheeks flushed. Her white shirt was untucked and hung over her pleated, tartan skirt, even her tie sat low around her neck. The grunge look suited the messy blonde hair framing her angular face.

"Who's interviewing?"

I glanced back down, still short a thousand words to finish my homework. Mr. Bloise threatened to have anyone in his history class who didn't meet the deadline write a longer essay. And of course, it would be about the most boring topic on the planet.

"The cops! Are you even listening?"

I closed my laptop and met her worried look. Then her words sunk through me like ice.

"Shit!"

"Did you get a request too?" She flopped down on my

bed, waving a piece of paper in her hand. "What am I going to do?"

Unease unfurled in my stomach, and I glanced at the door, where any messages I received slid into my room.

"Nothing."

"So, it's anyone who knew him?" She hugged herself, the paper scrunching up under her arm.

I joined her on the bed and dragged her into my arms, hugging her. "You'll be okay. This must be just normal procedures." What if my notification hadn't arrived yet, or they'd arrest me once they found my accomplice? My mouth was parched, and the ache in my stomach deepened.

"We didn't do anything wrong," I whispered.

Her face paled. "Only stuffed him in the basement and didn't tell anyone."

The words turned over in my head. She had a point, and I breathed deeply to calm myself because I'd been trying to get on with normal school, pretending it never happened. Ridiculous because a body lay at the bottom of this building.

"We need to move him," I suggested, lowering my voice.

Her eyes flew wider. "Not with the cops here."

"Of course not. But we need a place that's not connected to us." Unease shuddered through me for the poor sucker who'd lost his life, the family who worried about him, and then there was the real killer still out there. Or killers. Would the cat gang really stoop this low? All for the sake of harming me?

And why? Because I stared at her boyfriend the wrong way?

Ava whimpered and I hugged her tighter before dragging us both to our feet. "We did nothing wrong," I kept telling her. "And when they ask you, just tell them everything you knew about Drew. See if you can find out some details about who might have wanted to harm him."

She nodded, smiling. "Yes. Good plan."

I broke our hug and figured I'd pop back to my room during lunch and sneak in more of the essay. Plus, I also had an hour free after Rites and Rituals this morning.

So, I looped an arm around Ava's and we headed outside, making our way downstairs. After a quick pit stop at the vending machine to grab myself three blood bottles, we headed to class while I guzzled down my meal. Ava didn't react once, and even wiped a droplet of red from my chin.

Rather than the gymnasium, Mr. Gomez held his class outside underneath an enormous oak tree with low hanging branches. A cool breeze swished through my hair, and I appreciated him picking a shady location. "Today," he began, "We're splitting everyone up into groups."

Ava and I exchanged quick fearful glances. Yep, I didn't want to be paired up with anyone else in the class but Ava.

"Each group will receive instructions on the ritual to perform, and it's about working as a team." The wind buffeted his purple cape which billowed behind him as if he might take off into the air at any moment, his long, beaded necklace not moving, as if unaffected by the weather. He was tall and broad, and for the life of me, I couldn't work out what supernatural creature he was, but his eyes... they were as dark as the deepest pits of hell. Or at least what I'd imagined them to be. He leaned on his cane, while in his other hand he held a bunch of yellow notes the size of postcards.

"Judas, Bond, Nero, Ava. You're in group one. Please band together," Mr. Gomez said, and Ava seized my hand, squeezing it. The cat gang were eyeing my friend like prey. Damn, petty bitches.

How the hell did Judas and his two betas get to stick together anyway? They were high fiving each other, bumping chests, while Ava gave me a strange look of sorrow as if wishing it was me selected for their group. Part of me wished it was the case too.

She leaned over and whispered in my ear, "I'll try to get the dirt on Judas for ya."

Panic seized me at what she might accidently say, but before I could grab her arm, she slipped out of my grasp and sauntered toward the three predators. None of them paid her heed, but rather studied me, waiting for hell knew what.

Their eyes lingered on me, only on me, and I felt their heaviness. Their chests rising and falling deeply. Had I missed something?

My stomach gurgled from breakfast, though I bet it had everything to do with being in this situation.

"Here you go." Mr. Gomez stepped between us, handing Judas one of the notes. "Read it as a team and determine where you'll hold your ritual. We regroup in an hour."

The wolves broke into howls, and Ava glanced back my way, grinning. A fiery blaze spread through my chest. I'd have to be completely dead if I said I wasn't slightly jealous, especially when the guy with long, chestnut hair falling halfway down his back and the palest blue eyes, started chatting with Ava. Yep, all of them were so damn hot, and only now that I studied them, the sun illuminating their faces, did I see how deliciously gorgeous they were. Tanned, built with strong muscles, they were a perfect package. Wonder if they dated as a trio because whoever that girl was, she'd be the luckiest female in the world.

Judas glanced my way and winked. Heat seared over my flesh.

*I'm not jealous.*

*Not one bit.*

It was better this way. I didn't need Wolf complications in my life.

"Morwenna," Mr. Gomez called out, and I cringed.

Sniggers broke out instantaneously from the remaining students. The ground should open up right now and swallow me whole.

With a deep exhale, I approached the teacher and collected the note from his hand, as he called out the rest of my group. "Brylee, Salome, and Nesrin."

*Oh, come on. This wasn't fair.*

Three cat bitches pranced forward, hips swinging, wearing their Cheshire grins, filled with venom. And dread crawled over my skin because this class event was going to suck for me. And while part of me contemplated unleashing my fangs and taking them out, then I'd end up sentenced to death. Very tempting though.

Yep, I was cursed. I always stood up for myself, but now I just wanted to curl up under a rock and be left alone, to stop fighting.

Ava got sexy wolves, and I received bitches ready to scratch out my eyes. No wonder my stomach hurt worse. I didn't want to do this class now or ever.

I glanced up at the teacher, imploring for him to change our groups with my gaze alone, but he patted my shoulder.

"Better go and review your ritual with your team."

I grumbled under my breath as he called out the next group, but Nesrin interrupted him by shoving her hand into the air. "Oh Sir, can we do ours some place different. The old church is so wonderful for this."

"Um, I don't agree." I grabbed my waist, glaring at them.

"Doesn't seem fair," Judas interrupted, and I was stunned. He was standing up for me?

Mr. Gomez hushed everyone with a wave of his hand. "Majority rules, so get started. Remember, this is a team assignment."

I almost wobbled on my feet. With those few words, I'd been outvoted by three feline shifters to run a ritual in a goddamn church. Why the hell did they have that on campus anyway?

"Let's go," the blonde, called Brylee said, her curls bouncing perfectly around her face and over her shoulders. Cat-like makeup curled around her eyes, emphasizing her green pupils, especially against her ashen skin.

So, I dragged my feet after them, away from the class and buildings, and headed into the woods, following a worn track. I glanced behind me at Ava, who laughed as she joined the three wolves, entering the forest in a different direction to us, happy as a loon.

"So, how are you enjoying Bestias Academy?" Brylee asked, almost sounding genuine. She fell back to walk alongside me as the others marched onward. She offered me an honest look, like she was interested.

I shrugged. "It's not what I expected." No Beverly Hills 90210 as I'd imagined, but more like Addams Family school, if it existed.

Nesrin chuckled with the other girl before saying, "What did the penis say to the condom?"

And I rolled my eyes because I'd heard the dick jokes all my life, and this was why I loathed my name.

"Cover me, I'm going in." The two of them in front burst out laughing, and the joke wasn't even that funny.

Brylee smiled but shook her head. Was she the nice one of the bunch?

I wanted to be anywhere but here, and I looked up into a blue sky that had no right being glorious.

"You wanna hear a joke about Judas' dick?" Nesrin continued, and I clenched my fists.

"Never mind, it's too long."

The brunette near Nesrin cackled so loud, several birds burst out of a nearby tree, startled.

I ground my jaw, ignoring them. Nothing I said would change the situation, but with each passing moment, I hated them more.

Half a dozen weiner jokes later, and we arrived in front of a decrepit wooden church. Narrow, the building stood lofty with a pointy roof, the windows shattered and broken.

The small porch dipped in the center from overuse, paint on the wall had mostly chipped away.

I swallowed hard. My head fogged over, and for a moment, my world spun around me, while my gut gurgled again. Yep, even my body resisted going in there. Vampires and churches didn't mix.

Nesrin and the pink haired girl rushed up the steps and pushed inside, their footsteps like stomping elephants.

"It's okay," Brylee said and headed inside.

But I struggled to get my legs to move. What would happen if I didn't complete this task? Fail the class? Dad would be informed, and we'd be back at square one. Me marrying demon boy.

Nesrin appeared in the doorway, leaning against the frame. "You chicken? It's just an old building."

Her words shouldn't have gotten to me, but my nape bristled, and I pictured myself ripping her throat wide open with my fangs.

But instead of showing her she'd won, I raised my chin and headed toward the church. The porch steps groaned under my boots, and when I entered a bright sunlit room, it felt as if someone had punched me right in the chest.

I gasped for air, filling my dusty lungs, staring at the walls covered in crosses. Pews filled the large room, with cupboards near the transept, covered in shadows. I curled my fists, fingernails digging into the fleshy part of my palms, anything to absorb some of the agony ripping through me.

The choking sensation smothered me, my muscles growing heavier, more sluggish.

But this place wasn't going to kill me.

It'd just hurt like a fucking bitch.

I turned the ring on my finger over and over. It protected me from the sun, but not completely from the holy grounds of this building.

And Nesrin knew this. She'd counted on it.

"Let's get this done," I hissed through clenched teeth.

"Agreed." She whirled on her heels to face me, her raven hair glistening beneath the sunlight pouring in from a broken window. But it shocked me to hear her agree to anything I said. I eyed her suspiciously, waiting for a smart ass comment, but nothing came.

We all moved to the front of the room. Cobwebs dangled from the corners, from the rafters overhead. The wooden church was tiny and even the jagged shards of glass still attached to the window frame remained unstained.

The building must have been used when this was a school just for wolf shifters... the beasts who clearly needed God's intervention to drive the devil out of them.

No one knew the truth of where Shifters and Vampires came from... the supernatural had always lived in this world, right from the beginning, but they remained in the shadows. Hidden as a means to control both sides. Humans from panicking and hunting us down, while for the supernatural hid to stop us from using mortals as snacks. Didn't always work, but better a few rogue beings than full out war between us and them.

The three girls sat down in a circle in the middle of the room, and I joined them in a shady spot away from the sun.

Salome, the third of the clan with short, pixie style pinkish hair, was rolling a green crystal over her fingers, over and over.

I patted my pockets, searching for the tourmaline stone. Mr. Gomez insisted it offered protection. I couldn't even remember where I'd put it.

Instead, I lifted the note from the teacher and cleared my throat. "Assemble the group—"

"Yeah, yeah, we know the drill," Salome droned. "Just let Nesrin take over. She knows what she's doing."

Gleefully proud of herself, Nesrin fought the smile splitting her lips and when she met my gaze, I saw the animal inside her. *The Panther.* Ready to attack, and if I wasn't worried before, now I struggled to keep myself still.

"Don't worry," Brylee said, putting her hand on my knee, then she flicked it back as if touching me burned her. And now I was starting to understand why Dad always hated shifters. I agreed wholeheartedly.

"It's a simple cleansing ritual," Salome added. "And like Mr. Gomez said, it's all about teamwork."

"Close your eyes." Nesrin's voice grew soft.

Everyone fell silent, obediently following her instructions.

Brylee and Salome took my hand and we joined in a circle. I kept my eyes slightly open. Call me untrusting.

"Clear your mind," she explained. "Imagine you're in a

forest, the sun overhead and a path in front of you. Begin to follow it."

No one opened their eyes, so I closed mine too. And let myself follow the meditation, anything to distract the burning sensation along my flesh, the deep ache in my stomach. Maybe the blood this morning was off, as I'd never reacted this way.

My fingers started to tingle, the sensation shooting up my arms in a heartbeat, and I flicked open my eyes. Something felt wrong.

Nesrin watched me, smirking, and her two minions got up, helping her to her feet.

I tried to move, but a splitting ache rushed over me as if someone had run me over with a truck, then backed up over me.

I couldn't move.

Not even a toe.

Fear bubbled inside me like an unstoppable snowball about to slam into me. My skin was on fire, and the earlier pain in my stomach now swept through me like a blade, slicing every part of me.

I held back the cry, the agony.

"What did you do to me?" I growled.

They laughed, and Nesrin stepped closer before crouching down to reach me at face level. She tilted her head from side to side. "Relax, it won't be long now." She rubbed her chin.

And I knew right away what she'd done. "You poisoned the blood in the vending machine?"

She fake yawned. "Dunno what you're talking about, Leech," she snarled the insult shifters used to degrade Vamps, but I'd never had anyone say it to me. "Looks like a case of a guilty conscience to me. All those ugly thoughts *twisting and turning.*"

I shook my head as her voice swept me away with the spell. I tried to hold on, tried to keep my thoughts in order. *It's about the body...the body in the basement.* "You thought I'd be kicked out. But that didn't happen, did it?" I winced and tried to swallow the pain. "So now you...now you try to kill me?"

She smiled widened, her eyes gleaming with delight, and she grabbed my hand, studying my ring. "So pretty. You know, I heard it takes a human sacrifice for each of these rings to be created."

"Don't you dare!" I cried out, panic scratching at my brain like rusted nails. I searched her face for any kind of remorse, but she was vacant, so hateful. Salome stared at me with disgust, while Brylee...she looked away, unable to watch. She held some hope.

"Brylee, please." But she didn't responded, just walked farther away.

They were going to kill me. Finish me off just as they had Drew.

Nesrin seized the ring on my middle finger and ripped it off, before dropping my lifeless arm. "The world will be better off with one less Vampire," she spat.

They all stood, no glancing back, and turned for the door. They just left with my ring. My lifeline.

I screamed, tears pooling in my eyes, but the cries went unheard. "Give me back my ring!"

But I sat alone, waiting for my feelings to come back to my body, to get out of here. Except the ray of sunlight inched ever so closer to me from the rising sun.

This will be my end.

No one would think those fucking bitches murdered me. It'd be blamed on an accident.

But Dad would know. He'd rip this Academy apart to find the truth.

It wouldn't help me.

I'd be long dead, vanquished from this world.

# CHAPTER NINE

## THY MUST NOT ASSOCIATE WITH WITCHES

Pain ripped through me, feeling returning to my body so fast, my head spun. But it came with pinpricks from hell, and heaviness sunk through me. Moving was a struggle, my limbs weighed a ton, but the sun was almost on me.

Wolf's blood.

That bitch wanted to kill me. No trying about it, and she'd stared at me with ice cold eyes. And I had no doubt in my mind who murdered Drew now.

I scanned the pews, finding the faint shadows spilling across a cupboard at the edge of the transept. I shoved out my hand and crawled, shoving my foot against the floorboards. A cramp raced across my middle. I cried out, bowing my spine and closing my eyes.

*Get to the cupboard.*

The words filled me as I opened my eyes once more. I shoved and clawed.

Heat burned across my arms.

Blisters broke out along my flesh, popping and oozing. Stinging so fucking much. I clenched my teeth.

"So...goddamn...gross."

I lowered my head, smacking against the wooden pew. Every inch felt like a mile. I sucked in a hard breath as agony ripped through my insides. I slammed a palm into the inch-thick dust and dragged my body through the filth.

They were just lucky I wasn't wearing Dior. I ground my jaw, then I'd *really be pissed.*

A *squeak* tore through the church, making me freeze. I scanned the darkness before catching black beady eyes in the corner. "Stay away from me and I'll stay away from you, *deal?*"

The rodent just watched as I shoved against the floor once more. A savage burn tore through my chest. I coughed, sending droplets of blood across my arms and the floor. I stared at the dark red mess and tried to still the shudder.

*I'm not going to make it.*

*Not going to see my Mom.*

*Not going to see Dad.*

*Or Ava...*

Tears blurred my sight, whimpers tore free as I kept on pushing, lifting my knees to drive the side of my shoe against the floor until I passed the edge of the long line of pews. The towering cupboard rose in front of me. If I could reach out...darkness would cover the tips if my fingers. But my arms trembled and shook, until my hand crashed back against the floor.

"If you're up there." I lifted my head to the bright light pouring through the windows. "If you're up there, then I could really use your help."

My lips trembled, the words nothing but a blubbering mess. But there was no answer...not from the glaring light and not from Him.

I lowered my head back against the dirt and the grime...and then crawled once more, until the top of my head sank into the blissful darkness. I reached up, nails buckling as I clawed the handle...and yanked.

The thick wooden door swung open, darkness waited, barely big enough for me to fit. The stench of old shoes wafted out, making me gag. Still I'd shoved, leaving a trail of ooze from the sores on my arms behind.

Cramps wracked my belly. I whimpered and heaved as the tainted blood raced through my system. I shoved my knees higher and shoved against the floor, drove my body inside the dusty old cupboard, and yanked the door closed.

Heavy breaths filled my ears, but it was dark...*it was dark*. Tears slipped along my cheeks as I wrapped my arms around my knees. I could still hear their laughter, still feel their hate. Fingers skimmed bare knuckles finding a mark where my ring used to be.

They wanted to kill me...

They wanted to frame me.

*Why?* Thick tears came with word. My body shuddered, throat thick, and sore. I'd die here...die in a filthy cupboard amongst the old and forgotten.

A sound came from outside. *Rat...just the rat*...until... "Mor?"

I jerked my head upright, tears raining down my cheeks. "Ava?"

"Mor!" Footsteps thundered sounded like a herd of elephants outside the cupboard.

I'd never been so grateful to hear that herd. The cupboard opened an inch, and faded light spilled in.

Her eyes widened at the sight. Lips parted with a tortuous sound.

"Close the door, Ava!" I whimpered.

Air buffeted my face as it was slammed shut once more.

*"What the Hell is wrong with your face?"*

I bared my teeth at the question. "They took my ring...Ava they took my ring, and they poisoned me."

There was a second of silence. "What do you mean they poisoned you?"

"The vial...the blood. It's tainted."

Footsteps echoed again, before her voice came at the door once more. "What do you need...what I can do?"

I didn't know...without my ring I'd die out there—a tremor tore through my body. It might be pointless...maybe I was dying anyway. "Just...just stay with me. I don't want to go...alone."

"No way," her snarl pressed against the door. "You're not dying on me, Mor. I just fucking found you, and you're not leaving me now."

I pressed a trembling hand to the cupboard wall.

*Chuck.* I shoved to the side and grabbed my phone, my fingers trembling. The thing slipped in my hand. "Ava...my phone. Chuck can help me."

"I have to open the door, you ready for that?"

I closed my eyes and pressed my face into the back while I whimpered. "Okay."

She was a blur, just a flash of light before the cell was gone. "What's your password?"

"Dylan," I answered.

"Dylan? Who the Hell is Dylan...*nevermind. Not the time Ava.*" I listened to the tiny *click* as the lock gave way. She muttered when she concentrated. I closed my eyes as fire burned through my chest.

"It's ringing," she muttered, followed with. "Shit. Chuck it's Ava, Mor's friend. She's in trouble, and we need you like *now*. Call me back on this number."

She went silent for a second.

And the second passed into minutes.

She tried again...and again. Every message getting more and more frantic until she was almost screaming down the phone. I shook my head. "He's not coming. He'd pick up if he was...he'd be *here.*"

"Don't you give up on me." There was no bite of anger now in her words, just a solemn plea.

I could feel the fire consuming me as the tainted blood raced through my system. "It's okay," I whispered. "It's okay."

Footsteps echoed as I lay my head back against the side of the cupboard. And it was...ninety-nine years old was way too young to die as a Vampire.

But as a mortal, living in Beverly Hills 90210 it'd been forever.

I watched every season, *hungered* for every episode.

I pretended that it was *my* life, all the good times, all the dances.

And the fun times we had.

I closed my eyes as a cough ripped through my chest. Wet spittle hit my arms. I didn't care anymore. I tried to suck in a breath...tried to hold on for one last...second.

"*Where is she?*" The roar punctured the haze.

But it wasn't Chuck. It was...Judas.

"In the cupboard over there," Ava cried.

Her words were thick and distorted. The door was yanked open, silver eyes blazed like a knife severing the air. Savage and fueled with hate. "We need to move her!"

The door was slammed shut once more. My world tilted, rocking me backwards until my head slammed against the wood. I tried to lift my arms...tried to stay steady as I was rocked from side to side.

Screams came from outside the wardrobe. Ava and Judas. Savage snarls of Wolves.

Wolves who were my enemies, and in a gust of wind the door was thrown open. But this time there was no glaring sunlight burning my skin.

There was only darkness. I blinked as hands found me.

"I've got you," the words whispered in my ear.

I fell into him, hands slapping his arms before they fell away. He was all around me...my waist...my mouth...his hands brushed away my hair as he looked into my eyes. "They stole your ring?"

Tears fell as I nodded.

"Fucking bitches." Venom spilled from his lips. "The tainted blood, do you know what it was."

Pain savaged my chest at the thought. There was only one thing that could cause this.

Only one that was toxic to Vampires...enough to kill them, and the Panther had confirmed it.

I nodded. My words a whisper. "Werewolf blood."

He flinched and then pulled away. There was a second where he was silent...where words failed him, until he turned his head. Every single one of them had devastation in their eyes.

"Do you...do you know anything about this?" he murmured.

"Hell no," Nero snarled.

Bond just shook his head. "We'd never do that. You know us."

There was a nod before he glanced at my face. "I had to ask."

"Now that we know what's caused it, how do we fix this?" Ava murmured standing behind them.

Judas turned to me. "Any suggestions?"

I just shook my head. "Blood...powerful blood."

"We're out of the equation then," he murmured. "We can carry her."

"What? Through all the blinding sunlight we just passed?" Ava threw her hands in the air. "It's midday out there, she'll be crispy before we make it out the damn door."

The thought made me cringe.

"I'll do it," she declared.

My breaths stilled. I found Ava in the dark. "No, Ava. It won't work," I murmured.

She dragged her hands to her hips. "Why?"

"I love you for wanting to help. But I need powerful blood."

"I *have* powerful blood," she growled. "I'm the Princess of the Great Creatures of the Sea."

I stilled. The wolves stilled, and then we all turned our heads toward her.

She took a step closer, lowered her hand and shoved out her wrist toward me. "So, do it. Take what you need."

I looked to Judas who just shrugged. "What do we have to lose?"

Only my life...right? I was only aware of werewolf being toxic to my kind.

The frantic thunder of her pulse called to me. I stared at her exposed wrist and felt the pointed tips of my fangs. "I don't know how."

"What do you mean you don't know how?" Judas muttered. "How to what? Drink from a vein?"

My tongue pressed against thick fangs as tears spilled free. I could only nod.

"It's true, she's not like a normal Vamp," Ava came to my defense.

"You can say that again." Judas brushed my hair from

my shoulders and stared into my eyes. "Okay, so I don't know veins, but I know flesh. I'll walk you through it okay?"

I felt pathetic sitting here with oozing sores and fangs that ran over my lips. "But what if I hurt her?"

Ava knelt in front of me, drawing my gaze. "You won't. I don't think you'd know how. But I promise to tell you if you do, okay?"

I just stared at her, this weird girl who'd somehow become the best friend I'd ever had. "Okay."

"Now, take her wrist and place it to your lips," Judas murmured, watching as I lifted my hand, my fingers wrapped around the small, fragile bones.

Instinct raged inside me. I could hear Judas speaking as I close my eyes, but I was transfixed by that *thud...thud...thud...*in her veins. Warm flesh met my lips. I was already opening my mouth, already finding that jumping beat with the tip of my tongue.

"Okay, now all you have to do is—"

I opened my mouth wider and struck. Ava's tiny gasp filled my ears as warmth flooded me. So warm...so alive. It was liquid sunlight spilling down my blistered throat, slipping through ruptured veins.

I drank greedy gulps, taking draw after draw as I opened my eyes and stared up at her.

Her eyes were wide, breath panting. I tasted her breath, tasted her food...tasted...*salt*.

The sickening taste filled me, like she was coated with it. I opened my mouth, yanked my fangs from her veins and coughed and spluttered, dragging the back of my hand along my tongue. "OMG. Gross...what the hell is that? Did you drink the entire sea, or something?"

Ava slapped her wrist to her chest and rubbed the spot

I'd bitten her. "*You're welcome.* And I told you I was from the Great Creatures of the Sea."

She was almost pouting. I licked my lips as power flowed through me. Warmth danced across my skin, and as I watched, the sores slowly disappeared. Power roared through me, like the draw of a tide under a full moon sky. I shuddered with the energy, my bones vibrated, veins sang. I licked my lips once more and sucked in a hard breath. "Holy shit. It's like lightning."

"Just wait. You haven't gotten the full effect yet," Ava murmured.

I opened my eyes to find her. "What creature?"

"W-what?" she stuttered.

But she heard, I saw the panic in her eyes. "You said Great Creatures of the Sea, not Creatures of the Great Sea, so you must be powerful, right?"

She wrenched her gaze toward the wolves as they just stared at her.

"So...what creature?"

Her lips moved, and yet all I heard was a mutter. I shook my head. "I can't hear you."

"Kraken, *okay?* I'm a goddamn Kraken!" She threw her hands into the air again.

"Hollyyyyeeee shit." Judas' eyes widened. *"For real?"*

"For real," she growled and wrapped her arms around her middle, and in an instant her brown eyes gave way to grey. I knew she was something...but I didn't know she was *that* something.

And the Wolves were smitten. Their eyes sparkled with excitement. She was, after all, a rarity and I was an everyday boring Vampire...only the daughter of the most powerful Vampire in the city.

"That is fucking *awesome!*" Nero smiled wide and looked to Bond.

"Your home is far away, right?" Judas turned to her. "It's why you stay here when we all get to go home. Must've been a massive transition...Bestias."

"No...not really."

"So why did you come? I mean, we all had different reasons. What's yours?" Judas asked.

Her face burned bright red, grey eyes seemed to spark with danger. She wrenched her gaze toward me, eyes pleading. I had to save her. "I'm sure it's something boring, *right?* Me? I embarrassed my family for the last time, it's my own special brand of hilariousness."

I shoved against the floor, feeling my body sway a little more than it should. Inside, I was churning and rushing like the turbulent sea.

"Yeah? What's that?" Judas turned on me, his voice deep and insistent, and in the corner of my eyes I caught relief sweep through Ava's gaze.

"I call myself a penis."

Judas stilled, the other Wolves followed. "You *what?*"

"*I...call...myself...a....penis.*" I straightened my spine. "When my Mom wants to introduce me to important people, I call myself weiner, short for my full name. Morwenna."

"*No.*" Judas eyes widened until they bulged out of his head. "You don't."

"Why do you think I'm here?" I wobbled until I found my sea legs. "I introduced myself to some schmuck Vampire Lord called Hermond, and as punishment Daddy sent me here."

"See?" Judas turned to the others grinning. "*I told you she was crazy!*"

They smiled, looking at me, and for a second I was swept up in the excitement. Desire raced through me, but this was no remnant of Kraken blood...this was all mine.

Until Dad's voice filled my head. *They're our enemy. Mor. They'll always be our enemy...*

Enemy. The word was a bucket of ice water to the flare of heat racing through me.

"So now she's...not oozing everywhere, what do we do now?" Ava glanced to the doorway. "We still need to get her out of here."

"Is Ava's blood strong enough to get you to the dorm? It's closer than the infirmary." Judas took a step closer, unaware that my father's warning filled my head.

I nodded, swallowing hard as my head went to war with my heart.

"Okay." He reached out and skimmed the back of his finger along my cheek. "We cover her with the blankets on the window. I'll carry her and run as fast as I can."

"I can walk on my own," I muttered as my face grew warm.

"You really want to risk tripping and the sheet falling off?" He moved closer. "You think I'm not strong enough, is that it?"

I shook my head, words failed me now as the warm blush consumed my face.

"I won't falter, not with you in my arms."

His seductive growl drew me in. I found myself leaning into his touch and nodding. "Okay."

"Once I know you're safe, I'll find your ring," he murmured, staring into my eyes. "I promise."

"*We'll* find your ring." Ava growled. "Together."

My hands started shaking, my arms and knees followed like a million volts raced through me.

"It's starting, isn't it?" Ava watched me.

"I feel...like I'm going to explode." I stared at my trembling hands.

"Then we need to hurry," She looked to the wolves. "You *do not* want her here a second longer. Or she'll tear this place apart."

One nod was all she needed. Judas turned to me in an instant. He stepped close, bending down to sweep one hand under my knees, and the other at the small of my back. "Ready boys?"

They moved fast, striding over to the windows covered with thick heavy drapes. I saw the room then, the musty empty storage room. One yank of the canvas, and the dust burdened fabric fell over my head.

"Be still now," Judas murmured in my ear as hands ran along my body, tucking and smoothing until there wasn't a slither of light left behind.

I grabbed Judas' arm as we moved. Heavy steps echoed around me. I closed my eyes, ready for the pain and the light.

Hinges howled, seizing me with the sound, until the canvas sheet smashed against my face. My body rocked, hard, short movements, as the wind roared in my ears.

A grunt tore through Judas' chest as he drove his boots into the soil and we climbed. I pressed my face to the sound and his arms tightened around me.

No light found me, and no pain followed.

In this moment I was safe in his arms.

Safe in the arms of an enemy.

The musky scent filled me, sending warmth to places it shouldn't. I turned my head as we crested the rise and his thunderous steps smoothed, pressing my lips against the hard swell of his chest. "Thank you,' I whispered. "Thank you for taking care of me."

I'd had servants. I'd had guards.

But they were obligated to my father, and some were scared. But Judas was neither of those, he didn't care about climbing the ladder of power behind my father like Thorin. He only cared about me.

The screech of hinges sounded again. Only these were different. These ones I knew. Boots thundered on hard stairs, and in an instant, we were inside, and the familiar scent of my room surrounded me.

Tears filled my eyes. I didn't think I'd breathe the musky scent of old mattresses again, or hear the voices of those I loved. I thought I'd die there, in that musty old cupboard with last centuries shoes. Curtains were drawn, hard jagged breaths pressed Judas' chest against me...and for a second, I didn't want this filthy old sheet to move.

I wanted to stay here, in his arms...forever.

But the fairytale was stolen by the rustle of canvas and the feel of warm hands as Nero and Bond unwrapped me. Nero brushed the hair from my face as Bond ran his hands along my legs, pushing my skirt higher against my thighs. "She looks perfect to me," he murmured, his eyes never moving from the slide of his hand.

"That's enough," Judas commanded.

And the beta wolf obeyed, his hand falling from my skin. Still, I held onto Judas, staring up into his perfect brown eyes, as I pursed my lips and closed my eyes.

"Are you going to sneeze?" Ava muttered, and then snorted. "'Cause I am."

I opened my eyes. The perfect moment ruined by *where-choo...where-choo...where-choo.*

I jerked and jolted as Judas laughed, and lowered my feet to the floor.

"It's the dust." Ava flailed her hand in the air as her eyes watered. "I'm allergic to dust."

But all I could do was look at Judas, and then the other two wolves as they moved close. The three of them did more than save my life. They profoundly changed me. These were not my enemies...they were my friends.

They were more than that...

"Stay inside," Judas murmured.

"We'll find your ring," Nero followed.

Bond gave a nod. "We'll protect you."

"Nice," Ava snarled and then sneezed once more. "I'll just tag along then, shall I?"

Bond gave her a cheeky smile. "You *Kraken*, are powerful enough to do anything you fucking want to do."

She stilled, her eyes glinting with his words. Her hand fell away from a bright red nose, and even though her eyes watered she gave a nod. "Then let's go kick some Panther butt."

# CHAPTER TEN

## WOLVES AND VAMPIRES DO NOT MIX

I wrapped my arms around my middle.

They'd left me here.

Left me with my father's words ringing inside my head.

Left me with lightning racing through my veins.

My knee bounced and jerked and jiggled. I couldn't sit here, not while they were out there. I shoved my hand against the mattress and stood. My muscles were twitching, fingers dancing in the air. I needed to do something...*but what?* I kicked the dusty canvas sheet and strode into the bathroom.

The mop bucket sat in the corner. Muscles tensed. Nerves twitched. One pulsed and jumped near the corner of my eye. "Do something...or go insane."

Ava's blood was powerful. Very different from anything I'd had before. "Not regular 'ol type A that's for sure."

I turned my head, catching the mess of the canvas sheet in the middle of my room. I couldn't have it, not in my room. Not anywhere. I strode back in, twitchy fingers reaching out to grasp the corner of the sheet before I walked to my door.

I grabbed the door handle and inched it open, taking a

look at the shadows. Sunlight speared into the dorm, splashing against only one side. If I kept to the right, I'd be fine. My body was on fire, burning with the energy rolling around inside me.

I needed to work, so I jerked my gaze to the cleaning door at the end of the hallway and then stepped out. The rest of the dorm was quiet, most of the students in class. Would they notice me missing?

The thought stayed with me as I hurried to the cupboard at the end of the hall. I yanked open the door, folded the dusty sheet and put it on a shelf before grabbing a bucket, cleaning rags, and disinfectant...and then one more bottle before heading back to my room.

I scrubbed the bathroom, starting with the basin and the shower, using the rhythmic action to steal away my worries, and then I started on the floor.

The tiles gleamed as I bent down on hands and knees and scrubbed. Before I knew it, I was into the bedroom, heaving the spare, unmade bed into the air with one hand while I dusted and wiped. The steel frame gleamed with a swipe of the cloth and the air was filled with that fresh smell once more.

I didn't think about my ring as I cleaned. I didn't care about my nails.

Didn't worry about anything other than the motion of my hands, and the feel of *doing something*.

I was out of my room before I knew, staring down the landing to the foyer. Dust motes floated in the air. I could see them landing, see the filth left behind. I grabbed the bucket and the cloth and kept to the shadows as I made my way to the foyer.

Sweat broke out along my brow as I sank to my hands and knees once more. I scrubbed and shoved, moving aside sofas and cabinets to clean skirting boards and walls...until the place was spotless.

Still I twitched and scanned the foyer, stopping at the vending machine. The same machine which held tainted blood. I walked toward it, placing my hand on the gleaming glass I'd just cleaned.

But it wasn't the blood which drew me, it was the chocolate...rows and rows of chocolate. I grabbed my student card and swiped, punching the button for the biggest mint chocolate bar I could and watched it topple to the bottom.

I reached in, grabbed it and yanked it free, tearing off the wrapper with one savage bite. Sweet, chewy goodness filled my mouth before I swallowed.

"Mmm." So good. I bit, and swiped my card again, punching the buttons for another bar.

Before I knew it the pile in front of me was all gone.

The door opened and closed behind me.

"You've got to be kidding?"

I turned, chewing the half a bar still in my mouth and lifted my gaze to Ava and the Wolves. "What?"

Judas glanced to the machine, and then stepped closer. "How much chocolate have you eaten?"

I shook my head. "Dunno," I said, and then stared at the mess of wrappers all around me. "A bit."

Ava bent beside me and snatched the card from the floor. "Your card's almost worn out."

I stilled as fire lashed my insides, and with a belch, that fire reached a little higher. I grabbed my stomach, bit of nuts fell from my mouth as I lifted my head. "I don't feel so good."

"No wonder, you just ate your damn weight in carbs,"

Ava muttered and bent down. "I know you're a Vampire and all, but you really have to watch the damn calories."

I stared into her eyes as she grabbed my arm and slid it around her shoulders. "Didyougetit?'

"Did I get *tit?*" she studied my lips and then my eyes. "Oh, *did I get it? You had a bit of*...never mind."

A high-pitched screech came from Nero. "*Yeah...we did.*" He had his hand between his thighs, holding on to his balls.

I lifted my gaze to his face, only then did I really see them. All four had blood smears across their faces. Ava's hair was a tangled mess of knots, her uniform was dirty and a skewed. But it was the Wolves who had it bad.

Judas had a deep gash on the side of his neck. A gash that was already healing. And if it took this long to heal on a Wolf in the prime of his life...then how bad was it before? The sight was enough to sober me from a chocolate induced high. I straightened, sliding my arm from around Ava's shoulders and asked. "What the hell happened?"

Judas shook his head. "It's not important. Only this is." He reached out, and unfurled his fingers.

My heart leapt at the sight of my ring in the middle of his palm. I jerked my gaze to his. "My ring." I stumbled forward, grasped the weight from his hand and slipped it onto my finger. "Thank you...thank you all so much."

Power rushed as the sigil slipped into place. I sucked in a hard breath as the slight tremble raced through my bones. I could feel it, the strength from the witch's spell. Only one way to know for sure.

I took a step toward the gold rays of sunlight and reached out. Warmth touched the tips of my fingers and consumed my hand. I moved deeper, letting the golden rays reach along my arms, but this time there was no blistering and burning. This time, the stench of my own incinerating flesh didn't make my stomach churn.

I think it was the last ten chocolate bars.

Ava bent and grabbed my arm. "Okay, now we've established you're not going to go *poof* anytime soon, we need to get you up to bed."

My stomach rolled, and the room went with it. "Ugh."

"Okay," Ava muttered. "To bed with you."

"What about class and Mr. Gomez?"

"We've taken care of it," was all Judas said.

We left the Wolves behind and slowly climbed the stairs. I glanced at her, staring at her sandy blonde hair. "You know, you're really pretty."

"Now I just know you're drunk on chocolate," she muttered and ground her jaw as she heaved me up one stair after another. We stumbled along the landing and into my room.

"Look how clean it is." My words were slurred. "So pretty."

Ava steered me around and eased me onto the bed. My head hit the pillow with a rush, one arm flopped out as Ava bent, grabbed my feet and hauled them onto the bed.

"You didn't tell us."

She straightened, and met my gaze, brushing the knotted blonde strands from her face. "Tell you what?"

"Why you came here."

She wouldn't meet my gaze. Not for a long time. Her jaw flexed, her lips moved. She seemed to be arguing with herself, and then took a long hard breath and met my gaze. "I'll tell you on one condition."

I was riveted, and shoved up on an elbow. "Okay."

"You can't hate me. You have to understand it was an accident, and I hate myself for it every day."

I shoved until I sat upright, and crossed my feet. "This sounds bad."

She nodded. "It is."

I steeled my resolve, suddenly sober as a damn Gargoyle. "Tell me."

"I...I ate Derek."

I didn't think I heard right. *She ate Derek?* "Who the hell is Derek?"

She looked away. "He's my boyfriend...I mean *was...was* my boyfriend. I don't know what happened, one minute we were kissing and he was moving too fast and I told him to slow down. I told him that he was going too fast, but I was into it and he was into it, and then..."

"—and then?" I urged, gripped by this story. "*And then what?*"

Her eyes shone as she answered. "And then he grabbed my breast. I couldn't stop it. My beast, she just came out and ate him."

"You...ate...your...boyfriend, because he grabbed your boobie?" I couldn't believe it. I mean, even I'd been felt up by the handsy dead mortal hidden in the basement. But to *eat someone?* The words stayed with me like a bone I couldn't swallow.

And she just looked at me like she'd murdered an entire litter of puppies.

"You ate your boyfriend."

She nodded.

"Because he copped a feel."

The nod turned urgent.

There was a tremor in my belly, but this time it wasn't from sugar laden goodness. "Hmph." I tried to stifle the sound...and failed.

Laughter spilled from my lips, massive hawking laughter until I couldn't draw breath.

The room grew bright until I saw stars in my eyes. Still, I could stop, grabbing my belly as I whimpered and howled, rolling around on the bed. "Now...now I've heard it all. HEY EVERYONE! DON'T TOUCH AVA'S BOOBIES—"

She lunged, slapping a hand across my mouth, stifling the words. "Not another freaking word, Mor."

I stilled and flopped backwards onto the bed, and Ava came with me, we rolled and tussled, as I giggled and moaned with the torture until we lay in a jumbled mess. "Oh my God, I've heard some sex stories...but that...that one's the best."

I looked at her, quiet, staring into my eyes and she murmured, "I told him to stop."

I giggled.

She smiled.

And the smile grew wider, until she was giggling as well. "He tasted Goddamn awful too."

And a fresh wave of hysteria followed.

"I'm so glad Chuck didn't pick up, can you imagine if he found out what happened?" Ava muttered as she stared up at the ceiling.

"If he found out what?" The chilling growl came from the edge of my bed.

I shoved upright, smacking into Ava as she did the same. Cold, chilling rage lingered in his gaze. He was close to the killing edge...as close as any Vampire I'd seen before.

He jerked his head toward Ava and held up his phone. "Care to explain."

"So," she murmured, forcing a smile. "Funny story about that..."

# CHAPTER ELEVEN

## DO NOT EMBARRASS THY FAMILY NAME

I WANTED TO CRY.

A hard knot formed in my stomach as I stared up at Chuck. Ava clutched my arm, both of us sitting in my bed, pressed side to side.

His eyebrows were knitted together in a glare, while he held up his cell. The screen was black, but he referred to the ten panicked messages Ava had left on his inbox.

"Geez," Ava started, her voice shaky. "For a protector, you sure took your sweet ass time coming." Her forced laugh fooled no one, especially Chuck.

He'd been taught by the best. There wasn't a person he couldn't break...immortal, or otherwise.

But I wasn't just a person.

I was a Livingstone.

"I'll only ask one more time," he barked, his eyes narrowing as he judged me. "What happened?"

His gaze cut to my face, my neck, my arms. I'd never seen Chuck lose control, but that silent fierceness was terrifying.

I smirked and pushed my legs off the edge of the bed,

then got on my feet. Always face an argument standing, Dad would say. Take power away from the opponent, he'd insist. I stood tall in front of my guard and lifted my chin.

"I'm going to be honest here. It's like Ava said." I shrugged. "We were bored and wanted to see how quick you'd respond." I didn't need him running to Daddy Dearest.

God, could you imagine?

"I'm here to help, Morwenna. You can tell me anything." But beneath his voice I heard the warning. Step out of line and Dad would come down on me like a ton of bricks.

I rolled my eyes.

Before he could respond, I turned my back to him and strode toward the open door of the balcony. I wasn't about to be pushed around. Not now.

I'd found real friends who stood by my side. I'd not lose them now, even if three of those friends were considered enemies of my kind.

"It was nothing, okay? I had a mishap, and it's been taken care of. Daddy wanted me to learn how to stand on my own, so I'm learning. Anyway...if I was really in trouble, I'd be dead. What took you so long?"

I didn't turn around, but stared out into the daylight, letting the sun splash on my face. Blood smears filled my head. I lowered my gaze to the ring on my hand. We were safe, and okay... For now.

The graze on Ava's face had healed, and I was sure the sore set of balls Nero was holding had eased. But they'd fought to return my ring to me...when my official protector was nowhere to be found.

"I was called for an urgent meeting with your father. I came as soon as I could."

I turned then, staring up at the six foot four mountain of muscle and fangs. "What kind of urgent meeting?"

He flinched at the direct question. I don't think I'd ever been so bold.

"There's been talk of...*reshuffling*." Calculated, stony words hit me. My breath stilled, as I searched his gaze. Something was happening.

Something big enough to pull him away from guarding me.

Something that made him on edge.

*Reshuffling*...what did that even mean?

"They took my ring," I murmured. "These bitches took my ring, but we got it back."

His eyes widened.

"I'm okay, look." I lifted my arms, pale, perfect skin shone under the sun. "I'm perfectly fine. Ava and I handled it."

No way was I telling him about the three towering Wolves that helped me.

He glanced to Ava who just smiled sweetly and gave him a nod. "Good as new."

The ring glinted on my finger as I lifted my hand. "Daddy doesn't need to know about this, okay?"

He said nothing.

"*Okay, Chuck?*" I growled and took a step closer.

"Okay," he answered slowly, holding my gaze.

But relief didn't sweep through me. Instead, fear moved in.

"As long as you're safe here." His eyes bore into mine.

I faked a smile. "I'm safe, believe me, no one's gonna grab our boobies when Ava's around."

"*Mor!*" Ava screeched.

"Do I even want to know what that means?" he snarled and cut Ava a glare. "Has someone *touched you?*"

My stomach dropped. "No...*God no,*" I stuttered, as the phantom touch of Bond's hand skimmed my thigh.

"No one's touched her." Ava shoved from the bed to stand beside me. "And they won't either. I have boots...and I know how to kick a dick."

There was a twitch of his lips, the corner curling for an instant as he answered. "That's...good to know."

Ava just nodded and crossed her arms, standing shoulder to shoulder like we were ready to take over the world. "I got this." She gave him a nod.

He took a step toward the balcony and shoved the curtains aside. Did he believe our dance around the truth?

"Chuck...you believe us, right?"

But he just slapped a massive hand on the edge the bannister and leapt without answering.

"*Chuck!*" I roared, watching him tear across the Academy grounds.

"Well, I think that went well."

I glared at Ava over my shoulder. "In what world did that go well?"

She just gave a shrug. Yep, we were fucked.

The room spun, tilting on its axis. I jerked out a hand, searching for anything.

"Whoa." Ava grabbed my arm, holding me upright. "Think you need to get some rest."

I stumbled back in the room and flopped onto the bed before hugging my knees.

The mattress dipped and Ava brushed hair from my face. "If he does find out...what's the worst thing your dad could do?"

I thought about that for a second. Worst for me, or worst for everyone?

I turned my head, thinking of all the beautiful old buildings in the Academy Daddy Dearest would raze to the ground if he knew had what happened, and I shuddered.

I closed my eyes. It could've been a bed of thorns and I wouldn't have cared. I dozed and then surfaced, clawing my way through the nightmare where I was still in that cupboard, still screaming...screaming...*screaming*.

Until I woke with a jolt.

The room dark.

And still.

*Thud...thud...thud...*

I pressed fingers to my chest as that lifeless muscle squeezed and clenched driving nothing but fear through my veins. A *snap* came from the bushes outside. I shoved against the mattress, listening.

My senses buzzed, that heavy beat in my chest echoed in my ears. But underneath it was that aching...that desperation to be...something more.

*Snap.*

I wrenched my gaze to the window and dragged in a heavy breath. Someone was out there, someone musky and feral... I slid my feet from the bed and walked barefoot to the door. One twist of the handle and the night rushed in.

Shadows shifted at the edge of my sight, down there outside the dorm, something moved amongst the trees.

I clenched my jaw and took a step. Movement jerked my gaze left. Fear danced along my skin. But I wouldn't let it win, not this time...I curled my fingers around the edge of the bannister, and with one smooth jump, I launched over.

I hit the ground with barely a sound and scanned the dark before I moved. Toes sunk into soft earth as I skirted the bushes at the edge of the building and made for the whisper of movement.

It was just like a hunt...only this time, *it was real.*

Real hunger.

Real death.

Real fangs that nipped the soft skin of my lip.

And real blood, tasting like metal and tang against my tongue. I lowered my head, drove bare feet into the ground, tearing through the trees until they were a blur, and then lunged.

I hit him hard, grasped his shirt before we rolled and slammed into the ground. We tumbled in a blur, rolling in sticks and leaves before we both shoved to stand at the edge of the clearing. One eye bathed in silver, the other in the dark, the moonlight falling on the side of his face.

"Mor," Bond growled in a warning.

Thick white fangs glistened for second before perfect lips slid down.

I sucked in a breath, scanning the trees to his right. "What are you doing here?"

"Protecting you," came the deep growl behind me.

I turned, catching Judas stride from the corner of the building.

"She's fast." Nero said from the opposite side, closing me in.

"Protecting me from what?" I murmured and glanced from one wolf to the other, stilling on the Alpha.

Judas gave a shrug. "Everything."

"Shit, she was fast." Nero sucked in a hard breath, eying me suspiciously.

"I never heard her, not until she was right on top of me," Bond growled.

"You, Vampire." Judas pointed at me. "Are fucking terrifying."

I sucked in a breath, my senses on fire. "You scared the shit out of me."

"Thought you'd sleep through the night. We didn't want you vulnerable," Bond muttered.

Nero glanced toward the Alpha. "It was his idea."

And in a rush, something else replaced the fear.

Something soft and warm.

Something comforting.

"You were here for me?" I murmured.

One nod from the Alpha was all I needed. Desire surged from the terror that'd gripped me a second before. I stepped closer, and reaching out, seeking touch.

Judas moved first, sliding his arms under mine, his warm chest against me. "You're safe with us, Vampire."

Bond came from the side, one hand pressed against my back, as Nero closed us in, completing the perfect embrace. Here I was warm. Here I was protected. Here I was with friends.

---

"ARE YOU COMING FOR BREAKFAST?" Ava stood in my doorway, gripping a handful of books in her arms, pressed to her chest. "You're not even dressed yet."

I adjusted the towel wrapped around me, searching for my Transformations text amid the mountain of other books. I'd barely slept a wink from worry, and when I did sleep, my dreams were filled with shadows chasing me off the campus grounds.

"Need a hand? Class starts in five."

"Gah." I shoved papers and books aside finding nothing,

then I spied the pile near the bed. "You go, I'll catch up. Can you grab me a blood latte?"

"You got it."

I glanced at her. What? No nose scrunching this time? I was impressed.

I shooed her out of my room, closing the door behind her and rushing to get dressed. I clasped the buttons on the pleated skirt that fell halfway down my thighs. I yanked on my blouse before buttoning. I dragged a comb through my hair and stepped into my black shoes. Yep, no time for styling my hair today.

I rushed out of my room, down the stairs and out of the dorm in a flurry of panic. Students already rushing for first class of the day. I searched for Ava, catching sight of a group milling outside the main building in the middle of the footpath.

Two male students turned, pointing at something behind me. I glanced over my shoulder, tripping over a pothole in the ground and barely caught myself. Books slipped from my fingers. I clawed the edges, catching their fall...just in time, when my gaze fell on a familiar face storming toward me from the front building.

*Dad!*

Excitement flared for a second...before it came crashing down.

He swung his arms in his black pinstripe suit. His face a mask of rage. I knew that look...knew it well.

I clutched the books in front of me as my insides turned to water.

Chuck marched alongside him.

And Principle Stone just rushed behind, heels clattering on the pavement as panic gripped her features.

"You've got to be fucking kidding me," I muttered to

myself as I searched the yard for an escape.

Running had been my first instinct. But instead, I couldn't move, drawn back to those emotionless eyes and that ground eating stride. This was going to be bad.

"Morwenna," he called my name, using *that* voice.

The voice that scattered the servants.

The voice that made even Chuck wince.

"Daddy," I answered cautiously, eyeing Chuck and then Principal Stone. "What are you doing here?"

"The more immediate question should be, what *are you* doing here," he growled.

Panic was setting in... *Don't freak out...don't freak out...* "Ah, I go to school here, remember?"

"Go to school, yes. Study and learn, not be subject to *bullying*. Your ring." He shoved his hand out...waiting.

I swallowed hard and looked at Chuck, but he refused to meet my gaze, instead staring off into the distance. *Figures.* Principal Stone was no help, jerking her gaze from my Father to me.

I stepped, holding out my hand for him to inspect and felt his fingers close around mine like a vise. "Those who took it from you. I want their names Morwenna...*now.*" He glanced up meeting my gaze, still bending over.

I pulled my hand away, no matter how big and tough he might be to everyone else...to me he was Dad. "Not going to happen."

One brow rose in an instant. "I beg your pardon."

I swallowed hard, my voice now a hiss of air. "I said, not going to happen."

"As I was saying," Principal Stone gushed. "We have a lot of children from important families here, Mr. Livingstone. Some you very well may know, and there'll always be disagreements between students."

He turned on her like a Viper with its kill. "Disagreements? My daughter's ring was ripped from her, Principal Stone. An act that's akin to murder."

"We seem to be rife with that at the moment," she muttered under her breath, lifting her gaze.

I followed her focus, catching the men in suits at the edge of the field, pointing in the direction of the teacher's cottage and then the dorms. We'd found the prints at the crime scene...and now the catty bitches knew I was onto them they were praying for something like this to happen.

First, they framed me for murder, and then when that didn't work, they'd tried to kill me.

They thought they were getting away with it.

They thought wrong.

I took a step closer, sliding the books into one hand and wrapping the other around my Dad's waist. "Thank you for coming to my rescue. I love you for that." I lifted my head to meet his gaze. "But I can't give you what you want. I have to do this on my own, and I need you to trust that I can do this." I trembled all over, but I held myself strong.

No showing weakness.

Always face your opponent, Dad would say. And I did that, even if it was him I confronted.

Movement from the corner of my eye stole my focus. I straightened as Ava ran awkwardly toward me, the blood latte splashing the sides of the clear cup with every thud.

I took a step away from Dad. "I have friends now, Daddy. Real friends, and I can't...no, *I won't let them down.*" I hated how much my voice shook when I needed to him. I had control. Full control of my life; I no longer needed him to babysit me.

"You were attacked," Dad roared. "Say the word and I'll have you out of this school in the blink of an eye."

Movement at the corner of my eye drew my gaze. Nesrin stumbled and ran after a powerfully built man with the most stunning long black hair I'd ever seen. Rage drove every ground eating stride as he made for the main school building.

"Daddy, *please*," Nesrin whimpered and reached for his hand. He snatched it from her grasp, turning on a dime. The deep, feral snarl that rippled through the air made my father still and the hairs in the back of my neck stand on end.

Dark eyes glinted as Dad waited for my answer. Even though his gaze never shifted, he was aware of every movement of male Panther.

But it was the terrifying way Nesrin's father towered over her, making her cower like a scared little kitty... Looked like I wasn't the only one with Daddy issues.

"Morwenna," Dad growled impatiently.

I shook my head. Had he just given me the option to stay? And I jumped on that opportunity in a heartbeat. "I can't, I have unfinished business here, and besides, I'll be home next week. I have lessons and exams. And a..." *A murder to solve. Wolves that won't leave my thoughts.* "Answers to find."

The terrifying look in his gaze softened. "Your mother is worried."

"I know." I sighed, well aware I'd be grilled about school, about the attack. "But I have to stay here until semester is done, but I'll be home...."

"For your Reckoning," he added with a glint in his eye.

"And then I'll have my head in a book studying the Ancients. But right now, I want to make friends." I reached behind me as Ava stepped closer.

The bell sounded, making Principal Stone wince.

But my father said nothing, only glanced to Ava and then settling on me before he spoke once more. "Very well. But Chuck will no longer be confined to the edge of the school grounds. *He will* accompany you to all classes and all...other events."

I flinched at the command, my stomach hardening, before Dad glared at Principal Stone until she visibly quivered.

And in an instant, he turned and strode away...leaving me with one terrified thought.

*How the Hell was I going to find out who framed me now?*

# CHAPTER TWELVE

## FAMILY TIES CAN BIND YOU FROM WRONG CHOICES

"The body," I muttered, watching my father disappear around the corner of the main building.

"And the Wolves," Ava added, lifting her hand. The sound of slurping filled my ears, followed with heaving and retching as she realised she was drinking *my drink*. "*Oh my God,*" she howled. "This is so fucking gross."

I reached out, taking the cup of blood from her hand and shoved the straw into my mouth as my father disappeared around the corner of the main building.

Ava shuddered and shook, swiping her mouth and her tongue, still staring at the corner of the building.

"We have to figure this out, Ava." I turned to her, taking a long draw of my latte. "Before this gets worse."

She dropped her hand and nodded. "We need evidence," she murmured. "Real evidence against the cat gang, then we go to the police."

I turned to face the dorm. "Before we're through with them they'll wish they'd never even heard of Bestias Academy."

We made our way to class. It wasn't long before the

heady thud of footsteps echoed behind me. I didn't have to turn my head to know who it was, and my gut clenched.

I had a shadow now, a six foot four stony faced Vampire who was tasked to haunt my every move.

Last minute stragglers still milled in the hallways, some yanking items from their lockers as Ava and I shoved through the double doors and marched toward our classroom, clutching books against our chest.

Wolves, Ghouls, and a guy with gorgeous green eyes who smelled like the sea froze as we passed. Their eyes widening as they settled on Chuck.

Ava gave a heart-filled, heavy sigh. I turned, caught her tight smile, and rolled my eyes.

It looked like one of us was more annoyed with our tail than the other.

She jutted her chin in the air and marched past the gawking kids like she'd just made Prom Queen and Chuck was her King. I swallowed a groan and drank the last of my blood latte before throwing the cup in the bin outside the classroom.

Ava pushed through the door, and I followed, scanning the faces before I caught Judas, Nero, and Bond.

The Alpha turned, eyes shining as he found me, his lips curling into a smile. There was a vacant seat right next to him. His bag thrown casually across the desk. He motioned to the seat, reaching over to grab the straps of his pack and yanked it clear.

But I couldn't sit with him, no matter how much I wanted to.

I just gave a small shake of my head and watched the hope fade in his eyes before I stepped past, heading for a vacant seat at the rear of the classroom.

Pain followed, tearing through my chest as Ava slipped

into the seat that'd been saved for me and Chuck followed me to the back of the room.

I tossed my bag onto the desk and slumped into the seat, hating the world right now. Ava cast a pain-filled glance my way and mouthed the words, *sorry*.

I wrenched my gaze to the front of the class as Mr. Henesy raised his hand with the dull roar.

"Okay, come on now. Quieten down. Yes, we all see the...Vampire bodyguard in the room. Unfortunately, a few events have transpired in the last few days and Mr...." He looked to Chuck, who met Mr. Henesy's smile with a chilling stare.

"Mr. Guard," the teacher continued. "Is here for added protection."

"I heard he works for the mob," one of the other kids called out. "Better watch out." He cut a glare my way. "I bet it won't be a horse head you find in your bed. I bet it'll be a wolf's."

He glanced to Judas, who sneered. Anger turned honey brown eyes to cold, hard earth. There was a flare of his jaw, and the motion was mirrored in the two wolves at his back.

"That's enough," Mr. Henesy barked. "There's no *beheading* in this class. We're here to talk about one thing..." He pointed to the scrawl on the board behind him. "How to live in a Human world."

There was a collective groan. I stared at the front of the class as the teacher droned. He could be giving the *How to Kill a Vampire for Dummies,* lecture for all I cared.

My mind was elsewhere.

Judas glanced over his shoulder at me before he turned back to the front.

Nero followed.

And so did Bond.

I wanted to meet their gazes.

*Ached* to meet their gazes.

Instead I bore a hole into the whiteboard with my stare and waited for this damn torture to end. I scribbled in my book, avoiding the many glances from Ava and the Wolves. But there was only one glance I wanted to capture, and when Nesrin turned, I seized her gaze in mine.

She curled those full lips into a pouted sneer and then glanced at the ring on my finger. The others had come back bleeding, limping and talking in an unusually high pitched voice. But she didn't have a damn hair out of place. Brylee smiled sweetly, and Salome leaned against the back of her seat. Like they hadn't a damn thing to worry about.

But they did...they'd set me up and tried to kill me.

And I was making it my mission to prove it.

The bell rang and I moved with the rest of the class, grabbing my pack and striding from the class. Chuck watched my every move, even when I tried to step close to Judas and whisper in his ear.

So, I just kept on moving through the next class...and then at break, avoiding his glances at every opportunity until finally the shrill sound of the last bell rang for the day.

Ava fell in step as I headed for the dorm. "That was painful," she leaned close and whispered.

"Not as much for you as it was for me," I muttered and curled my lips at the echo of Chuck's step behind me.

All my life I'd listened to that sure-footed, heavy gait and never given it a second thought.

But today the sound wore at me like a broken nail.

Ava shoved through the door to our dorm, and that last heavy thud of his boots drove me over the edge. I spun and lifted my gaze, trying hard to keep the sting from my tone. "No, not inside. I draw the line at that. There's one way in and one way out. I *need* at least a sliver of privacy, Chuck...*please.*"

He stared at me and then lifted his gaze to the foyer behind me. I wasn't asking him to break the rules...just bend them a little.

One slow nod of his head made that fist around my heart ease just a little. "I'll be right here then," he murmured.

The way he said it made me feel like an ass. "Thank you." My tone softened before I turned and slipped through the door behind Ava.

She was already at the top of the stairs, striding toward her room before I caught her muttering, "I was looking forward to luring him in with my charms tonight."

The sullen pout almost made me chuckle. "I've heard all about you luring men in with your charms. I'd like to have my bodyguard alive after all this is done."

She shoved her key into the lock on her door and smiled. "That's fair."

"Anyway, I've got other plans for tonight."

And in an instant, I was the center of her attention. "I'm going downstairs."

She glanced toward the foyer.

"No." I motioned my head toward the door at the end of the hallway. "I'm...going...*down...stairs.*"

Her brows narrowed, for a second before an, "Oh." The whites of her eyes shone. "You're going *down stairs.*"

I nodded.

"Why?"

I glanced toward the front door of the foyer and took a step closer keeping my voice low. "Cause, I think we need to look at *it* again."

Both brows rose this time. "Oh, you sure about that, given how squeamish you are?"

In this moment, me being squeamish was the least of my problems. I felt like I'd lived a hundred years in the few weeks I'd been at Bestias Academy. This version of me was stronger, determined and less squeamish than before. "I'm sure."

"Okay, let me change and I'll be in."

I turned to my door, shoved the key into the lock and stepped inside. My thoughts were filled with basements and bodies and hulking Vampire guards who watched my every move.

Until they turned to Judas, Nero, and Bond.

These guys didn't understand my father... Or the level of hatred he had for their kind. There might be an uneasy truce between the Ancients, even though the Wolves and Vampires had been at war for thousands of years, but to my father there was no truce at all. He held onto the past, listened to the Ancients, their fear mongering.

And the remnant of that hatred lingered inside me.

But Judas, Nero, and Bond were different. They weren't the killers Dad told me they'd be. They'd helped me, protected me. I opened my cupboard and dragged a pair of black jeans free as the feel of Judas's arms rose to the surface of my thoughts.

I looked to my ring, still hearing the heavy thud of his boots as he'd rushed through the woods to save me. Dad was wrong about them...I just had to figure out a way to prove it. I took off my skirt and stepped into my jeans, before changing the school blouse for something a little freer and pulling on black boots. Time seemed to pass slowly while I waited.

After grabbing my text books, I sat cross legged on the

bed and tried to flick through the pages, attempting to do something at least.

"You're such a fake," Ava muttered, glancing at the open books. "You have about as much concentration as me right now."

I closed the cover and shoved the textbook away. "You're right. I can't think about anything else. We need proof, Ava, and we need it before I return home."

"This birthday is important, isn't it?"

"The Reckoning of the Dead." I leaned against the pillows. "It's the day we get our assignment from the Ancient."

"Hunter, healer—"

"Theologian," I finished and met her gaze as flopped down onto the bed. "The Livingstone's have come from a long line of protectors, some more notorious than others. But Dad's praying this time it'll change. He doesn't want me out there fighting on the front line. He wants me safe with my nose in a book and my head in the past."

"A nerd?"

I took a long breath and signed. "Yep, a nerd."

"And is that what you want?"

I shook my head. "It doesn't matter what I want. Knowing my father, he'll have it all picked out, what I study, where I go...what I wear."

"Sounds more like a prison to me."

"Me too," I answered. "Me too."

We chatted about class and boys, about makeup and dresses and parties, leaving the hard reality of my future behind. Ava shifted and then turned to lay on her side. And even though we'd only just met, it felt like I'd known her my entire life.

She grabbed my hand and raised it into the air, fingers

entwined with the kind of love I'd always wanted. A sister's love...

"We need manicures," I muttered staring at my nails. "Before the party. We go all out, hair, makeup, Gucci dresses."

She snorted. "Gucci dresses? That's so not me."

"For my birthday it is. It's what I want, what's expected." I turned to the girl who forced me to be her friend. But there was no forcing now. "You're the best friend I never knew I wanted."

She smiled...a heartfelt smile. "I knew it the moment I saw you. I knew we'd be inseparable."

And as the sun dimmed and night moved in, I knew she was right. No matter what happened. I'd found someone who always had my back.

"It's time," she murmured, shoving up from the mattress. "The others will be busy, they won't even notice we've gone."

"You go down, check on Chuck, and then come back."

She slipped from the bed and nodded. "On it."

"And Ava..."

"Yeah?" She glanced at me over her shoulder.

"You know there's no future with someone like Chuck, right?"

"Yeah, I know." She gave me a cheeky smile. "A girl can dream though, right?" Her expression shifted as if a new thought popped into her mind. "And who said it had to be a long term thing anyway?"

"Eww, gross. Don't need those thoughts in my head about Chuck." He was like my father or brother...he was family.

I laughed as she opened the door and slipped from the

room. Ava and Chuck were not a match I'd like to think about, and it was more for his safety than it was for hers.

Minutes later, my bedroom door opened and closed, Ava now in my room. "We're good to go. I grabbed a flashlight this time."

"I don't need it, twenty-twenty vision." I tapped the side of my head. "Even in the dark."

"Fine, well I do," she muttered and held open the door.

I followed, closing the door behind me. I watched the hallway for movement as we raced toward the door for the basement. Music slipped out from under one of the bedroom doors, voices drifted from another. They were busy in their own world. I glanced toward Nesrin's room and found only darkness in the gap under door, it was the same with Brylee and Salome's.

They'd pushed me...and right now I was about push back.

Ava opened the door at the end of the hall and a second later the bright glare of a flashlight cut through the dark. I slipped in behind her and closed the door.

The bright beam swept through the dark expanse. Up here on the landing it looked like a whole different building. The musty smell of stagnant water and old things crawled inside my nose. Ava stepped to the side and motioned me forward.

"After you Ms. Twenty-twenty."

I gripped the bannister, feeling the tremble a little too deep. "Just because I can see what's coming at me, doesn't mean I want to be in the firing line."

"Too bad," she muttered. "You're it."

I eased down, step after step as the memory of the dead guy's hand returned to fondle my breast once more. I shuddered and crossed my arms as I finally hit the bottom and glanced around the place.

Boxes and towering junk lay under heavy draped. It seemed the place was used as storage....

"There it is," Ava muttered and aimed the beam over a box covered with a lid.

"Not sure I'm ready for this," I whispered under my breath.

"Hurry up will ya?" she muttered.

She pulled the lid off and a putrid stench slammed into us, smothering me.

"Eww." Ava recoiled, slapping a hand to her mouth.

I recoiled, gagging, convinced I'd never stop vomiting if I started. Someone had said once you smelled a dead body, you'd never forget the putrid odor.

One leg had slipped out of the wrapping, the sheet riding high on his thigh. A ghoulish outline that would haunt me forever.

"Gross," Ava grumbled.

I'd never be able to scrub that sight from my mind.

"We need to move it."

I gave her a glare. "You ready to do this?" I caught my breath and choked on the smell.

"I sure as Hell am *not* touching that thing again," she declared. The flare of blonde hair caught on the light as she shook her head and then turned to the corpse.

It looked like it was just me then. I stepped closer, reaching out to flick the corner of the sheet as silence settled around me. The eerie feeling made me twitchy. "Talk to me,"

I growled.

"About what?'

"I don't know...about your home...your family. Tell me about your family."

She sighed and then slowly started. "We don't have flashy stuff like this place where I come from. It's simple and quiet. We have a home that was once an old castle. You can hear the sound of the waves hitting the rocks from my bedroom. It's just me there. I had a brother but he's gone now."

"I'm sorry," I murmured and reached for the sheet again.

I listened to her talk about her family and her home. In my head I was painting a picture of green hills on one side and the deep blue sea on the other, but my eyes were seeing a very different picture.

Pasty pale skin, wide opaque eyes. I reached up and closed his eyes. I didn't want him staring at me, not while I...

The bites were purple and red and...*gaping*. I pressed my fingers to bloated flesh that had me gagging, finding the outline of a bite. And found something else.

Ava's voice droned as I moved closer, kneeling down in front of the body and moved to the next bite. It was the exact same, small punctures into the flesh. But just back from that, hidden under the torn skin from thick molars were two more punctures, only these drove thin, and deep, *deeper* than any animal bite.

I eased backwards. "A canine's bite didn't kill him."

"What?" Ava stopped mid sentence. "What do you mean, *canine didn't kill him*. It's feline...it's Nesrin...Nesrin and her bitches."

I rose from in front of the body and shook my head. This didn't make sense. "No, this bite is a Wolf's. Were the cats involved? Probably. But they didn't kill him...Something else did."

"What?" She took a step closer. "But I thought…"

Something clattered to the ground with a *crash* in the distance.

I jerked my gaze toward the sound as Ava let out a screech.

Footsteps echoed, coming this way.

I lifted my fists, catching the blur of movement as someone strode from the darkness and out into the bright beam of light as Ava grappled with the lid of the box and slapped it back over Drew's body.

"You know, for two people trying to be stealthy, you sure suck," Judas muttered.

"You need extra classes," Nero followed.

"Maybe we discuss some after hours tutoring?" Bond teased.

I spun at the sight, stepping in front of the box containing Drew, but there was nothing I could do about the horrific stench. Not even my entire bottle of Chanel No.5 could mask this stink. "What the Hell are you doing here?"

"Coming for you, silly." Judas glanced back the way they came. "Found an unused tunnel that ran from one basement to the other. The more important question is what are *you* doing here?" His nostrils flared, having caught a whiff of the body. "What…the…hell?"

Shit. Shit. Shit. I forced a smile as Ava just froze.

Judas' gaze slipped behind me to the box, icing over.

"Funny story," Ava muttered.

It seemed to be her go to line when she was nervous.

Judas jerked his gaze to me, dark brown eyes hardening. "I think you'd better tell us what the fuck is going on."

## CHAPTER THIRTEEN

### THY SHALL NOT LIE TO THE DEAD

"Is that…is that a body?" Bond lifted his chin, sniffing the air, eyeing the box with Drew stuffed inside. He made a disgusted noise and backed away. The other two did the same.

Ava winced, staring at me for an answer, and me… I felt sick to my stomach.

We were busted, and of all the people to find us, it had to be the Wolves.

*Please don't call the cops please don't call the cops.*

The putrid stench had me so faint that the room spun.

"Haha," Ava just laughed and then…*snorted.*

But no one responded, and we stood around in an awkward standoff. I wasn't fool enough to believe we'd lie our way out of this situation. We faced off with Were-wolves, and they knew exactly what the stink in the air belonged to.

I swallowed hard. "I've got something to tell you, but don't freak out."

Judas studied me, his eyes darkening. "What did you do?"

Ava broke out into a strangled laughter again. "We did nothing," she declared.

But I held Judas' gaze, well aware when we faced our match. "The body in the box is Drew. The human exchange from the Academy." I stiffened, waiting for his reaction.

His face blanched almost immediately, while Bond exhaled loudly, "Oh fuck!" Nero ran a hand down his face as if unable to believe his ears.

But I kept talking, fast, before they made up their minds I was the killer. "A week ago, I found him in my room. Just laying there, dead, covered in bite marks."

"It's true." Ava was nodding quickly. "I found Mor standing over the body in her room." She laughed louder, nervously. "Not like she killed him, but like... You know... She found the b...body." Hell, she was panicking.

Judas folded his arms over his chest, glaring at us. "Drew was a decent guy. He didn't deserve this."

I hugged myself around the middle to stop myself from trembling. I'd done nothing wrong, so I shouldn't be scared, but I was so fucking terrified. Drew lost his life for no reason other than for someone to incriminate me. So, I told the Wolves everything, ranting on and on about what Ava and I had seen and done. Including the paw prints near the teachers' cottage.

"You can check out the bites for yourself." Stepping back from the large wooden box, I welcomed the Wolves to inspect for themselves.

Bond scrunched his nose, while Nero stood there, unmoving.

Judas stepped forward, holding back his emotions, but I saw the way his shoulders curled, the way his spine bent slightly forward.

He wanted to run.

They all did.

And so did we.

Ava pressed against my side and we watched Judas peel the lid off, his head flinching back from the assault of smells. I covered my mouth with a hand. We needed to nail the lid shut forever.

No one said a word.

Judas bravely peered in and then he stuck his hand inside. The other two wolves joined him, suddenly finding their courage.

Ava and I stared at each other, unspoken words saying everything. Our fear. The urgent need to run. Were they Wolves going to report us?

The earlier sickness in my gut intensified.

When a loud bang sounded, I flinched up to see the three Wolves shutting the box before turning to us. Their eyes had morphed into wolf eyes, bright and predatory.

Where they furious, or hungry, or...My breaths refused to come. "I...it wasn't m...me. Someone is setting me up."

Ava stood tall next to me, and I knew that if the Wolves were to turn against us, she'd fight alongside me. Though I wasn't a fighter and didn't have my daggers with me.

"You're right." Judas' voice sliced through the silence. "Those are animal bites. It's got that barnyard stink."

"It's a shifter," Bond snarled. "Definitely."

"But I can't pinpoint what exactly," Nero added.

"A feline maybe?" Ava suggested.

They all shrugged but didn't dismiss the idea.

"It's unusual, like several smells blended into one." He huffed, his brows pulling together. "But the smell will only get worse. Someone will find Drew, and then they'll investigate everyone here."

"I know," I muttered. "That's why we hid him, but it looks like now we need to move him someplace else."

"Where?" Bond asked, his voice serious, his gaze judging us. But this was my first time dealing with hiding a body.

My mouth opened and then shut again because I hadn't thought out that far.

"The woods," Ava declared. "Maybe the river."

Bond's nose scrunched, his shoulders squaring. "Drew deserves more respect than that."

"Yeah, and so does Mor," Ava snapped back. "She's the one being framed."

"Agree with Bond," Nero stepped forward. "He needs a proper burial."

"What?" Ava said. "We're not looking to bury him. Just hide him a little. Simple."

"You're all right," I said, touching Ava's arm. Here I'd been so worried about myself, I had given little thought to Drew and his family. "We need to find somewhere to hold him for a while longer until we come up with a solution."

Judas nodded and turned to his pack. "Let's find a bigger box we can fit this one into as it might help conceal the smell." And they set off doing just that, while Ava and I stood there.

My chest ached from knowing that the wolves were involved, but at the same time I couldn't be happier to have them on our side. Something about sharing the load lifted the weight of the world off my shoulders. Yep, I was a walking contradiction.

Ava leaned in closer to me and whispered, "So you think we can trust them?"

"Don't think we have much choice, but I yeah I do trust them."

When I looked up, Judas met my intense gaze. He'd heard Ava; of course he would with his big Wolf ears and all.

With Drew boxed up in two layers of containers and shoved into a dark corner, the Wolves turned to us.

"We should leave," Nero suggested, his voice dark, already turning toward the entrance to the tunnels. Judas gave me a quick nod, but something behind his gaze left me feeling uneasy. Could I really trust him? What stopped him from reporting us?

His word?

I wanted to believe he'd be honest.

Nero stepped closer, his hand on mine, his thumb circling the back of my hand. "Everything will be alright. You can trust us." With a wink that captivated me, he drew me toward him, and for those few moments my thoughts took a back seat. I simply fell into his gaze, into the bluest eyes, loving the way he stared at me, a dimple appearing in his cheeks when he smiled like he knew something I didn't.

He released my hold, and my arm fell back by my side. "We'll speak tomorrow."

He spun and darted after his friends, vanishing into the shadows of the basement.

Ava took my hand and pulled me toward the door. "What the hell was that? You two googly eyeing each other. I thought you had a thing for Judas?"

"I don't know." Too terrified to voice that not only did I find Judas cute, but my stomach did somersaults around Bond and Nero as well, I kept my mouth shut. At least until I understood my own emotions.

We left in a hurry with my heart in my throat, uncertainty slithering down my spine, and with my hand tingling from Nero's touch.

THE NEXT FEW days flew past, and I kept my head down. Ava was at my side always, and each time we passed the Wolves, we exchanged knowing looks, but we kept going. We shared a secret that could get me killed and them expelled from the Academy. Maybe worse. I avoided Chuck too because, with each passing day, I kept worrying someone would discover Drew by the smell, and he'd see my worry, then put two and two together. It was bad enough Dad had marched onto campus, drawing everyone's attention.

The solution was to move Drew, I knew that, but we needed to do so without being spotted. Then, we'd focus on uncovering who killed him and get proof, meaning we could finally hand over Drew to his family for a proper burial.

I sighed. Not even my morning blood latte helped settle my stomach.

"Did you hear anything I said?" Ava gripped her hips, gawking at me. Behind her, the Academy bus was crammed with students. The sun shone brightly today, bringing on a mild headache that thrummed at the base of my skull.

I rolled my eyes. "Is this trip mandatory?"

"That's what I've been telling you. Whoever doesn't attend fails class."

I groaned loud enough to gain Mr. Henesy's glare. He wore a long coat that fell to his ankles and he could have easily stepped out of a mystery movie. All that was missing was a wide-brimmed hat.

"Livingstone and Blaine. On the bus, now."

Ava grabbed my hand and we climbed on. The chatter was close to deafening. Most seats were taken. The cat gang occupied the rear of the bus. I scanned the faces until I landed on Nero smiling at me. The other two Wolves sat behind him in conversation, but Ava dragged me to an empty seat near the front. On the bright side, no sign of Chuck. Had he forgotten about the trip? One could wish.

"This is going to be fun." Ava twisted in her seat to face me.

I somehow doubted that. "Can't remember the last time I visited a museum."

The bus lurched forward, shoving me back into my seat. Everyone hooted, including Ava, and I couldn't deny their excitement influenced me too. Being homeschooled didn't compare. I smiled widely and joined in because it felt amazing to be part of a group. I cheered and fell into laughter with Ava.

"All right," Mr. Henesy's voice boomed through the speakers, and I cringed as my headache worsened. "Now that everyone's settled, let's go over today's field task as there'll be a quiz on this."

Despite everyone booing, he kept going. "Your assignment isn't to admire the museum. But to study the Uniforms and learn how to live in a human world." He cleared his throat.

Uniforms.

It wasn't a word I'd heard in so long. It was mostly used by shifters referring to humans because they had one form, unlike them who could shift into two forms.

"Pay attention to how they interact. Their behavior. There will be several mortal schools attending today, so your assignment is to observe and take five things they do differently compared to the gifted like us."

Sounded easy. I'd watched enough Beverly 90210 to have observed dozens of human mannerisms.

An hour later, we pulled up in a parking area, and

everyone shoved and pushed to get off the bus. Ava nudged me to join the masses, and then someone pinched my ass.

I flinched and turned around to find Bond smirking right behind me. He'd always been the serious one of the three Wolves, but now he was someone else. A guy I couldn't stop admiring with his perfect jaw, the high cheek-bones, and the piercing blue eyes. They were almost glowing in the shadows of the bus.

"Hello." He smiled, teasing me, his stare changing to something more primal.

My chest was tight and I swallowed hard.

Ava had my arm and pulled me out of the bus. "What's up with you and those Wolves?"

He hopped out onto the sidewalk, and I glanced back as more students poured out like a river. But I searched for those blue eyes, and when they found me, my skin rippled as if someone had swept a feather over my arms.

I turned back to face Ava. "I don't know. But something happens when the three of them are near me."

She arched a brow. "Yeah, that's called hormones, girl."

I laughed and we turned toward the museum when my sights landed on Chuck, standing near the entrance like a guard. And I wasn't the only one who noticed. Most took a wide step around him because no one wanted to be near the terrifying Vamp.

When I passed him, he studied me, but I saw his eyes flicker to Ava, the tiny twitch at the corners of his mouth. Ava's breathing hitched.

Hell, those two better not get their hopes up because there was no way he was going to be with my friend. Especially after the stunt he pulled by reporting me to Dad. I wasn't ready to forgive him yet.

Ava and I headed inside where Mr. Henesy handed us

red wrist bands and waved for us to head through a dark hall into the museum.

We emerged into an enormous hall with lofty ceilings and some kind of dinosaur skeleton dangling overhead.

"Whoa." Ava stared at the remains, at the sheer size. A winding path encircled the walls, littered with kids running up and down to various levels and galleries they vanished into.

"Where do we start? I want to see everything here." Ava beamed, and before I could respond, she seized my hand and hauled me through the crowds. We pushed past mortals who grumbled and gave us filthy looks for shoving past them.

I looked behind us to see Chuck struggling to keep up and thought that maybe this wasn't such a bad plan.

The first room was a live re-enactment of a deadly earthquake, but I remembered our task for the day. Except, Ava was already in line and waving me over. Maybe a few fun activities, then we'd get serious.

Two hours of laughing and running around nonstop, feeling like a child, I couldn't quit smiling. When was the last time I'd giggled so much?

I spun around, searching for Ava, who'd darted to the next gallery, when a dark shape rushed toward me from within the crowd. Shadows fluttering behind it like a cape, and whoever it was wore a black mask.

It all happened so fast.

My smile faded and fear rushed through me.

I recoiled, jutted out an arm, the other reaching for my boot. But I didn't carry any knives with me. Not today.

A scream bellowed past my throat.

The shadow slammed into me.

Darkness.

Night.

Whatever the fuck it was, the thing was solid and moved like the wind.

And now darkness choked around me, blocking my view.

I punched and kicked and hissed.

My fangs snapped out, and hell, I might not know how to drink with them, but they were my weapon. We fought, arms and legs swinging, needing to get out from under the attacker, to pin them down.

Chaos broke out around us. Cries filled with terror and thundering footsteps rose. Someone hit an alarm and the blaring sound screamed overhead.

I sucked in the scent of salty sea mixed with a metallic tang. Just as I had in my room before I found Drew's body.

And realization hit me.

This was the fucker who killed him. I felt it in my bones. Whoever they were had come for me. Brazen *sonofabitch*, attacking me in daylight, in a busy place.

"Get off me!" I thrust every punch into its head, grabbing for fabric to rip away from their face, to reveal the culprit. But they were too fast.

A clawed hand jutted out from the cape.

I flinched but was too slow.

It scraped over my neck. A piercing ache stung like hell. I screamed again and again. Fear thumped in my chest as if I had a beating heart.

I faced death.

And adrenaline roared within my veins.

But like my hunt in the woods, a scorching power bubbled inside me. Raging. Pulsing. And it felt so fucking right.

I drove the power down my arms, buzzing over my flesh, and I thrust my palms into the attacker.

Jolting backward, she grunted.

*She.*

The sound belonged to a female behind the mask.

Chuck reared behind her, grabbing her shoulder and throwing her off, to vanish somewhere in the shadows.

I dragged myself backward on my ass, terrified, searching for a place to hide. Maybe a weapon.

But when a shadow fell over me, I raised my fists and hissed, but instead of Death, I found Chuck.

My savior.

My guard.

My family.

"She attacked me!" I screamed, searching the room for the shadow. The fear was thick in my throat, looping through me, invading my mind.

I almost died.

"Are you hurt."

I shook my head. Ava darted into the room, her eyes huge orbs of dread. She fell to her knees next to me.

Chuck swung around and darted to where he'd flung the attacker.

"You're bleeding." Ava tugged at her white shirt sleeve and in one heroic moment, ripped it away from the seam and pulled it off her arm in one tug.

"Holy shit!" I almost laughed at how ridiculously silly it looked, but instead tears blurred my eyes.

"You'll be okay." She folded the material over my neck.

Chuck was marching back toward us, his brow furrowed, hands fisted. No shadow in sight. We were inside a gallery decorated like the universe with stars overhead, oversized planets in every section of the room. Chuck looked out of place here. Like an alien who'd arrived to take over our world. Furious and relentless. But he was my savior. And as much as I'd hated having him around, I now cherished him being here.

I caught movement at the entrance to the room and found Judas, Bond, and Nero. They were terrified, their faces ashen, but when Judas stepped forward, I shook my head and glanced over at Chuck who now stood over me.

"I'm taking you home," was all he said.

"Like her room in the dorm, or home *home*," Ava asked.

But I knew what he meant. His answer lay deep in his furious voice.

I climbed to my feet, but he picked me up into his arms, cradling me like I was baby. "Put me down." My cheeks burned and I'd never hear the end of it from the cat gang and I sure as hell didn't want Judas and his Wolves to see me this way.

Wriggling in Chuck's embrace, he lowered me to my feet, and my gaze shot to the entrance, expecting to see the Wolves. But they weren't there. Only Mr. Henesy was, hands gripping his waist, worry twisting his expression.

"You can carry me if you prefer," Ava teased and grabbed my attention. She was fluttering her eyelids at Chuck, and I just didn't have it in me to bother with her flirting with my guard.

"Hello, I almost died," I reminded them.

Chuck straightened and placed his hand to my back. "Let's go."

At the door, I met the teacher's terrified gaze.

"He's going to take me home," I said. "I'm sure I'll be back." I prayed that was the case.

"And I'm going with them," Ava butted in. "They'll drop me off at the Academy. If Chuck doesn't mind?"

"We will?" I asked.

"Ava...come on, you can't die on me. I won't allow it," he said.

Her eyes popped open.

"Of course you can all leave," Mr. Henesy interjected and nodded nervously, his gaze never leaving Chuck's. "I will take care of this situation."

And we left the museum, merging into a crowd of students and panicked staff hovering outside the building. I held Ava's sleeve against my neck, pressing it tight to stop the bleeding. No one but those from our Academy would know the evacuation was because of me. Gossip spread like wildfire I bet.

I kept my head low, not wanting to meet the judging gazes. I'd prefer to crawl under a rock and never come out. When Dad found out, he'd lock me up in my room for my own protection. No going back to the Academy now, and I felt sick in my stomach. Fuck!

When we reached a black sedan with deeply tinted windows, Chuck opened the back door for me. I crawled inside. Away from the prying eyes. I hated how weak I felt in that moment. Instead of fighting because I was a fucking Vampire, I was bested by some shadow ninja.

Chuck shut the door, and I expected Ava to climb into the back with me, but instead she got into the front with Chuck.

I slouched in the back on my own. Not jealous, but curious. How would it really work between them two? He was a protector, Dad's minion, and so much older. Would Ava's parents even approve? She was from the sea folk. Her family and Vamps just didn't see eye to eye on things.

"So, back in the museum," Ava muttered, gazing over at Chuck like a love-struck teenager, which she was I guessed.

"What did you mean by *won't allow me to die?* Do tell, handsome."

"Ugh, enough you two."

I curled in my seat, holding the material to my wounded neck, and Chuck laughed as he started the engine. A rock song blared from the speakers, and I let myself fall into the lyrics. They sang about the world coming to end. Yep, it suited my situation perfectly.

By the time we pulled up into the Academy driveway, throbbing police lights had me jerking upright in my seat.

"What the hell?"

"Stay in the car, both of you," Chuck demanded and got out. He strolled toward Principal Stone who stood still as a statue, arms folded over her chest, staring out at the authorities.

"What do you think happened?" Ava asked.

I stared out at the students across the field, police and even firemen near our dorm. And my stomach dropped.

Ava and I exchanged terrified glances. "Do you think?" we asked in unison.

Chuck was running back to the vehicle and climbed in, the car groaning under his strength. "Probably a good thing you're coming home." He glanced over his shoulder at me.

But I couldn't move as my thoughts swam to Drew in the basement. I couldn't even let myself think the worst. Wouldn't, or I'd burst out crying with fear.

"A main water pipe burst in your building and the whole ground floor is flooded. They found a body in the basement." His voice hardened with that last part. Not in the kind where he glared at us for being responsible, but the kind that reiterated why Dad would never let me return to the Academy in a million years.

My veins turned to ice.

"Who was it?" I murmured while Ava bit her nails, blinking so fast I worried she might pop an eye.

Chuck shrugged. "Who knows. They'll probably want to interview everyone, but not today. You're coming home." He glanced over at Ava. "Are your parents nearby? I can drive you home."

She shook her head and reached for the door handle. "No. They're nowhere close." Half stepping out of the car, she looked back at me with fear in her eyes. "When will I see you again?"

I choked on my response, hating the pain in her gaze because it reflected how shattered I felt inside. How scared. How lost. And I was leaving her alone in this mess.

"I'll message you," was all I could offer.

She shut the door, then we were reversing, and leaving behind the Academy.

I had no idea what came next. When I'd see my friend again. Or the Wolf guys who had me melting in their presence, but most of all, I prayed I wouldn't be facing the firing squad any time soon.

## CHAPTER FOURTEEN

### THE ASSIGNMENT FROM AN ANCIENT IS A SACRED DUTY

"You awake?"

I opened my eyes to my father's voice. He hardly ever came into my room and never to wake me. I shoved up against the mattress and felt agony tear along my neck from my attack. "Yeah, you okay? What's wrong? Is it Mom?"

He reached out to touch the bandage, pain filled his eyes. "We're fine, just worried about you is all. I wanted to talk to you about that school."

"Oh, Dad," I groaned and flopped back against the pillows a little too hard. A wave of nausea swallowed me as the room spun. I fisted the sheets and closed my eyes, waiting for this sickening feeling to leave me.

But it wouldn't; it was here to stay.

"You'll be off studying in some foreign land soon, all the different supernatural creatures."

I opened my eyes. "I don't want to do this right now. If you bend me to your will any more, I swear one day I'll snap."

He flinched at the sting in my tone.

"Have you *ever* thought about what I wanted to do? Just

once...just one small second where you thought, *hey, I wonder what Mor wants to do WITH THE REST OF HER EXISTENCE?"*

I swallowed and rolled away, shoving the sheet aside and stumbling out of bed. "I have put you first all these years. I went to this party and that party and met this Vampire and *that* Vampire."

"And embarrassed us—"

I turned, my long night dress billowing. "Because I *hated it.* I hated the parties. I hated being the daughter of...of..."

"Of a murderer."

"Of someone who *never* put my needs above his own."

I'd never seen Dad in pain. Never seen him anything other than rock fucking steady. But now his shoulders slumped, head bowed. A shudder passed through his body before he clenched his fist, swallowing the tremor. "You think I was that selfish? I *only* thought of you. Thought how your life would be if you followed in my footsteps. I want better for you. Not this life of violence, of always watching over your shoulder." He lifted his gaze. "Terrified those you love will be taken from you."

I flinched with his words.

"So, if you felt like I was pushing you into something you didn't want, then I'm sorry...but I was. I want you to be away from here...and away from me. I wanted you some place you'd be safe, and if that's nose deep in the ancient texts of our kind then that makes me happy."

"Daddy," I started.

He rose from the bed and closed the distance between us. "I love you with all my heart, and even though I might have my doubts about this Bestias Academy... I have no doubts about a certain someone."

"That someone be me dawg." Ava sauntered into my room, staring around at the walk-in wardrobe and the expansive bathroom. "Holy shit, Mor. You live in a fucking palace!"

I winced.

Dad just smiled and shook his head. "Teenagers."

"I'm almost a hundred," I retorted as I threw open my arms and stumbled toward the gawking weirdo in the middle of my room.

I hit her like a linebacker, throwing my arms around her middle. "God, I missed you."

She just stood there, bound by my arms and answered, "I missed you too. The last few days have been utter torture. I'm now reduced to being 'that girl' in class again. They just don't appreciate my unique qualities like you do."

I pulled away, smiling. "No, they don't."

"Right, I'll just leave you to fuss and scream and get ready for the big celebration."

"Thanks Mr. Mobster... *I mean.* Mr. Livingstone."

I could hear my father still laughing as he walked out of my bedroom and down the hall. Ava burned bright red as I grabbed her hand and pulled her toward the king sized bed. "Tell me *everything.*"

"It was a bloody nightmare," she muttered. "We could hear Principal Stone screaming from our new dorm."

"New dorm?"

She nodded. "They moved us, all of us. Nesrin and the cat gang were *pissed,* until she realised that the dorm is the same as Judas and the Wolves. We have a full time guard to make sure there's no funny stuff. But boys and girls together."

My heart sank. "I bet she was excited about that."

Ava stifled a chuckle. "She was...right up until she met the new guard."

"Oh?" I met her gaze. "Who was that?"

"Her father," she answered with a snigger. "And he was *pissed*."

"I bet. He's coming to the party, you know."

Her gaze narrowed. "Really?"

"The Ancients sent a request to my father, apparently the heads of all the lines will be here."

"Except for the Sea people," she murmured.

There was an edge of disappointment in her tone. I reached out, grasped her hand. "I'm sorry. I wish it was different. Maybe one day we can change it, and have all the beasts combined as one."

She shook her head. "Dad would never allow it. He said the sea and the land creatures don't mix and never have. We're too salty, apparently." She gave a soft smile with the words. "Anyway, you promised me a manicure and I heard there's a Vamp place that is phenomenal."

"Caskets and Cravings," I answered. "I've heard of them, but I've never been."

"Well." She shoved to stand. "Get that ugly ass bandage off your head and let's get soaking." She waggled her fingers at me, and then motioned toward the wardrobe. "And FYI. I'm touching *all* your stuff."

I shoved away from the bed and laughed. The old me would've been mortified, all those bags, all those bracelets...all those diamonds. I strode toward the bathroom. "Have at it. But you stretch my jeans and I'll stab you with my freshly painted nails."

"With an ass like that there's no fear of stretching."

"Hey!" I spun and gave her a wink. "It's not that big."

She lifted a hand, smothered her mouth and pretended to cough. "Bullshit."

I just shook my head and walked into the bathroom. It was quiet in here without Helene fussing. But I didn't want her picking up after me, not anymore. It felt strange returning home, like I couldn't quite fall into step. The things I once took for granted now sat uneasy.

I didn't want a maid. I didn't want this life. I reached up and unwrapped the bandage from around my neck, staring at the fading mark on my flesh. Blood soaked bandages now lay in the bottom of the sink.

Fragments came to me, the deafening sound of shattering glass...the black blur before pain savaged the back of my head. Human scents and screams all around me. And I was back there, in the panic and the terror. A tortured sound escaped from my lips. I reached up to grasp my throat and closed my eyes.

"You okay in there?" Ava murmured.

I jerked my gaze to the doorway as I slipped from the past. "Yeah, *yes*. I'm all good."

"Excellent, this Hermes red leather jacket is so damn soft."

I tried to smile, but the happiness just wasn't there, not like it used to be. I stepped into the marble shower and hit the taps. The warm stream cascaded like a waterfall from the wall. I sank into the warmth, letting it run all over me until the ache melted away. I washed and scrubbed, lathering my skin with familiar scents of white lily and pear and then rinsed the bubbles out.

I could hear Ava talking as I hit the taps and ended the flow of water. Soft murmurs piqued my interest. I grabbed a towel, dried quickly and then wrapped my robe around my body.

"Oh, Chuck, you shouldn't say things like that, you'll make me blush."

*What...the...fuck?* Chuck was in my room? With my best friend?

"Oh, don't be silly, you big goof. Say, how old are you anyway?" Ava murmured trying to sound seductive.

I leaned closer to the door, craning to hear his deep growl.

But I heard nothing...not from him at least.

"Oh, Chuck," she murmured.

I gripped the handle and eased open the door just a crack. Ava stood in front of my mirror, kissing the damn thing. I stifled a giggle, she wasn't talking to the towering undead lump himself...*she was pretending to.*

"What's going on?" I asked quietly.

Ava jumped, let out a squeak and stumbled backwards, leaving lipstick smeared across the once gleaming surface.

"Nothing." Her face flushed. "Just looking at something."

I crossed my arms. "Mmmmhmmm."

There was a long sigh, before she turned and in a soft voice. "Look, I have something to tell you." She met my gaze and then looked away. "I like...*oh God this is embarrassing.* I like older guys."

"No shit," I muttered.

"I can't help it, it's just a thing that happens."

I glanced to my mirror. "So is leaving a film of kisses over my mirror."

She winced, reached up and attempted to smear the marks even more with the sleeve of my Hermes leather jacket. I just smiled and shook my head.

"Don't worry. I'm getting dressed and then we're out of here. Manicures and pedicures are calling."

I strode into the wardrobe, grabbing a pair of soft black jeans and a red t-shirt with the caption '*eye roll*' printed in the middle and tugged it over my bra.

"Okay," I muttered carrying a pair of heeled boots with me. "Ready?"

"Will Chuck be accompanying?" she started.

"*No,*" I muttered. "He's helping Dad with the celebration."

"I can't believe everyone is going to be there, and I get to see it all." She almost beamed.

And her smile was infectious, washing away the last of my doubts. "We have to go shopping." I yanked on my boots. "Get you something nice to wear."

"Something blue," she murmured. "Or green, or blue and green."

I just laughed as we strode toward the door.

***

"You sure this is the place," Ava murmured and stared through the tinted windows of the limousine.

"For the tenth time, yes. We don't have to go in if you don't want. I told you the place was run by Vampires."

"No, I'm okay...this is okay. I'm okay," she repeated and then met my gaze. "Don't you want dark sunglasses and a wide-brimmed hat? You're famous around here, right?"

I just laughed. "I don't think I'm famous, like I said I've never been here, and booked us under a secret name, *Ebony Black.*"

"Wow," she muttered and sighed. "Put a lot of thought

into that one I see. May as well announce, *I'm really important and shit with names.*"

I actually liked that name.

She yanked the handle and the door opened with a rush, making her fall forward. "What the fuck." My driver reached out, grasping her hand and catching her fall.

She just shook his waiting palm and then climbed out herself. "Thanks buddy, I'm good."

He glanced at me with a look of confusion as I accepted his grasp and climbed out a little more gracefully than my guest. She was all arms and legs, stumbling around like a newborn giraffe. "I just don't know." She glanced over her shoulder at me. "I mean...I've never been to a morgue before."

"They run the nail business from a room at the back." I headed for the rear of the building. "As far as I know it's perfectly fine."

***

"This does not look *perfectly* *fine to me*," Ava growled and eyed a covered body on a gurney up against the wall.

"Oh, I just *love* this place, Juliette," came a nasal voice behind us. "It's so quiet, I can actually have a conversation. I've got *soo* much to tell you."

I kept my gaze straight ahead as the receptionist ran a long, black pointed nail along a list of names. "Oh, here we are, *Ebony Black.*"

Ava let out a moan, until I jabbed her with my elbow. I'd met the receptionist's gaze three times now, and there wasn't a hint of recognition, not from her, or the nattering idiot behind me.

"Juliette, you need to hurry, gurl. I got a party to get ready for."

The receptionist smiled and laughed. "Raven, you've *always* got a party to get ready for. This way ladies."

I risked a glance at the Vampire over my shoulder. She was busy touching up her lipstick in the shine of the stainless steel mortuary refrigerator door.

"This party is different," she muttered, staring at herself. "This is *the* party. The one I've been waiting for."

"Okay, just pop off your shoes, soak your feet in the special formula in the footspa and I'll be with you in a jiffy."

I turned from the strange Vamp and followed Ava as the technician motioned to two leather seats and filled footspas with cloudy, pale blue water.

"Ah, what is this?" Ava stared at the water but the technician was already leaving, hurrying to the loudmouth at the front desk.

Giggles and chatter followed. Ava slipped off her shoes, took one look at me and then rolled up the bottom of her jeans before placing her feet into the liquid. "Oh, that's nice."

The chatty Vamp was taken to the chairs behind us in the large room. There were three other Vamps, already getting tended to by hunched over nail technicians who buffed and shone.

"You doing this or what?" Ava muttered.

I sat on the chair beside her, yanked off my boots and then pulled up the legs of my jeans. The other Vamp chatted and gossiped like she was the only one in the room.

"Leroy said he's going to get me an invite to the Livingstone party. I'm so excited. I cannot wait to see the moment they finally take that sonovabich down."

"Raven," Juliette hissed softly. "Not so loud."

"What?" The bitch was even louder. "We all know what he is...he's a murderer, the worst kind of murderer...he kills his own people...killed my Urden, he was the kindest man I ever met."

If my heart was working, blood would've drained from my face.

Ava jerked her gaze toward me, her eyes widening, lips curling. She reached out, grasped the armrests of the chairs and pushed to stand. I knew what she wanted to do...rage was written all over her face. I reached out, placed my hand over hers and shook my head. "Don't," I warned. "It's not worth it."

Anger burned Ava's face. She was going red enough for the both of us.

"I heard the Ancient is going to do it at the celebration, *dethrone the king*. I feel sorry for his family...heard his daughter's a bit of a stuck-up cow."

"That's it," Ava growled. Water splashed the floor as she kicked the spa. An eyeball bobbed to the surface, throwing her from her murderous intent. "*What the fuck is that!*"

All eyes turned to us.

I stared at the eyeball as Ava screamed and wailed. Juliette stopped fussing over the bigmouth and strode toward us. But it was the bigmouth I watched as she lifted her gaze, and for the first time saw me.

The Ancients were taking down the most dangerous Vampire in the city.

And they were doing it on my birthday.

Somehow, I knew this was all connected to the dead body in my room. I had no idea how, but it felt too much of a coincidence that someone had tried to kill me, no doubt in an attempt to make my dad suffer.

I reached out, grasped Ava's hand and snatched my boots from the floor and pulled my feet from the water. "Come on, we're leaving."

*"You're fucking lucky!"* Ava grabbed her shoes and roared at the back-stabbing bitch. "Imma knock those fangs outta your head."

"God you're embarrassing," I muttered, towing her behind me.

But I loved her more than ever before. No one had ever stood up for me, not like that...with fire and rage in her eyes. I softened my grasp, storming through the morgue toward the rear door of the building.

"Ms Black!" Juliette called behind me.

But we were already gone, punching through the door and striding out into the open to where the limousine waited. My bare feet slapped against the pavement, but I couldn't feel the burn. I was livid, and more than that...I was desperate.

If the Ancients were planning something for my birthday tonight, then Dad needed to know, and we needed to prepare not just for a birthday...but to not go down without a fight.

We were Livingstones...

We were family.

# CHAPTER FIFTEEN

## EVERY ACTION HAS A CONSEQUENCE

"Where's Dad?" I cried out to Helene, who flinched in the kitchen while holding a silver tray filled with deviled blood eggs. Those little suckers rolled back and forth, their deep ruby color calling me, looking rather delicious.

But I couldn't stomach anything right now. I rushed closer, unable to stand still, unable to forget what I'd overheard at the manicure joint.

"He won't answer his phone. Where is he?" I insisted.

"Mistress, is everything all right?" Her brow creased as she studied me with worry. "You've not changed yet. The guests are arriving soon, and your father will be furious if you're not ready."

"Have you seen him?" I hadn't meant to raise my voice, or clench my fists, but this was a matter of life and death. Not even Mom was anywhere to be found.

Ava stepped up alongside me, her breathing heavy as we'd run through the house, searching for my parents.

Helene shook her head and placed the tray down on the

counter. Ava approached the eggs, staring down at them, poking one as if it might roar back at her touch.

"You need to calm down. Today is your big day. And your father has everything under control."

"That's not what this is about, I have something urgent to tell him."

She tugged down on her pristine white apron. "He left with your mother an hour ago. They'll be back soon and you need to be dressed by then."

The doorbell rang and I jumped.

"Good, hopefully that's the stylist team. Your mother has booked you both in for hair and makeup."

I sighed, not having time for this. I chewed on a hang-nail, staring at Ava who kept prodding the blood eggs.

"Chuck. We need to see him then," I said, and Ava snapped around at once when I mentioned her crush.

"He went with your parents," Helene called out as she rushed toward the front door.

"Hell!"

"Mistress," Helene sang out from the living room. "The stylists are ready for you and Ava." Her tone held that firmness behind it, but I had to warn my dad, not sit there getting pretty.

Ava took my elbow. "Looks like we're getting made up. Once your parents return, we tell them everything. They'll fix the issue, and we might even be able to still celebrate your party. Win, win."

Maybe she was right. Not as if we could do anything until they returned, so I followed Ava into the living room.

An hour later, our hair had been curled at the ends, styled with diamond pins, and sprayed to stay in place. While I had my hair set, one of the stylists applied Ava's makeup, so the process didn't take long.

Now, I twirled in front of the mirror in my bedroom, unable to believe how stunning my dress looked. The blood-red, sleeveless gown was studded with hundreds of diamonds. It cinched in at my waist, giving me that perfect hourglass figure, while the satin fabric fell to my ankles. The diamonds glinted each time I moved. Givenchy gowns always looked amazing and this one matched the Bvlgari necklace I wore, adorning a dagger pendant made of rubies.

My dark hair cascaded over my shoulders in ringlets, a contrast against the red fabric, and exactly why I'd picked this color months ago when we ordered the dress.

"Damn girl, you look sick! No one's going to show up my girl at this party." Ava stood in my doorway, dressed in a black Gucci gown made of spider silk, with an oversized gold belt and buckle around her middle. Her heels were golden and strapped around her ankles.

"You look gorgeous," I said.

She strutted over, her red lips drawing into a smirk, and stood next to me. We were goddesses.

"Do you think Chuck will be impressed?"

I almost blurted out that she shouldn't get her hopes high for him, but with the way she smiled so brightly, I didn't want to bring her down. There was enough shit to deal with tonight, and if she wanted to daydream about my guard, then I wouldn't stand in her way.

"Mistress," Helene called out, rushing down the hall to my bedroom in a flurry. "Your guests are arriving."

"Shit. Are my parents here?" I bunched up the gown around my legs so I could take quicker steps. In my stilettos, I met her half way in the corridor. "Is Dad back?"

Ava's footsteps closed in behind me.

Helene shook her head. "I've not seen him, but you need to come." She turned and headed downstairs.

I'd planned this party for months. The gown, the theme, right down to the food, and the black steel daggers we'd use as cutlery. Only the best, right? That's what Dad had said. I chewed my bottom lip and glanced toward the doorway. No matter the glamour and the glitter, it was all for nothing if I didn't receive my assignment from the Ancient.

Every Vampire had a place...until tonight my place had been here at home, obeying my parents. Tonight, that was meant to change. Tonight, my father was supposed to get his way...and I'd become a blood-drinking nerd.

But now I had so many other things cluttering my mind. Drew's body uncovered in the Dorm, the cops wanting to probably interview me.

Would I get an assignment from the Ancient, or would I be killed too?

Dread, filled me.

My life felt out of control.

And I tried to keep it all together.

"You okay?" Ava took my hand in hers, palm to palm, she was as steady as the tide. "I'm with you, no matter what happens."

I turned around and hugged her, the diamonds on my dress rubbing against her gown, but I didn't care. I had a friend who understood, who remained by my side, who I'd dragged into my mess. "Thank you."

"We're a team. We'll face anything together."

And hearing those words meant the world to me. My throat clogged up, and I broke our hug before I started bawling my eyes out. But more than anything, a newfound strength surged through me, and I was ready to face whatever the universe dealt.

"Let's do this." We marched downstairs, the nerves in my stomach raging.

The party had been set up in our ballroom. A location my parents used for guests frequently as they entertained a lot.

"I'm so freaking nervous," Ava said. "And it's not even my party."

"Not sure I could eat a thing."

She cut me a surprised look. "Not even those blood egg things that looked ready to hatch a demon?"

I laughed so loud, mostly out of nerves, and we headed inside as two guards opened the double doors for us.

Upbeat violin music greeted us. A compromise I made with Dad who had wanted a harp; I said, over my dead body. So, we'd agreed on a modern violin band I found on the internet.

The ceiling was coated in red balloons, glitter filling them, with the intention of being popped later tonight when everyone was on the dancefloor, which currently had no one in it. The tables were set up with golden plates and cutlery, red roses. A large group of attendees were near the bar, boozing it up, and the rest stood around in small groups, enjoying the snacks being brought to them by waiters in black suits. The table in the far corner was already over-flowing with gifts. And I should be excited, but I was shaking.

I froze suddenly. No matter how many functions I attended, I tended to keep to myself.

Now, I was expected to greet them all. I wanted to turn and run, but Dad was in danger, so I'd mingle and find out what I could.

Before I could step forward, Thorin marched over, his chest sticking out, his eyes drinking me in, and his mouth curled into a smile. He wore slick tailored pants with a high collared black shirt, along with a deep red velvet coat that drew the eye to the lace like pattern running down his sleeves. Yep, he was going for the Dracula look all right. That's what I called those supernatural who adopted the gothic style; hair slick off his face, dark makeup around his eyes. The guy tried to fit in with the Vamps, I'd give him that.

"Spunk incoming at two o'clock," Ava stated the obvious.

I leaned closer and whispered, "He's a demon."

She gasped.

"Morwenna, dear." Thorin took my hand and bent at the waist before kissing the back of my hand. Several spectators turned to us, watching. "You look ravaging. The red brings out the paleness of your cheeks." His eyes fell to my pushed up cleavage. "Turning one hundred changes a girl into a woman."

"Nice of you to join our party." I ripped my hand from his grip, but he snatched it back and placed my palm over his hard chest.

"You break my heart with your tone."

Ava was clearing her throat loudly, and when I glanced around, I caught Judas' eyes on us, intensity behind them as he watched me with Thorin. Despite Dad loathing the Wolf packs, they were invited. As were other supernatural and Vampire clans.

But seeing Bond and Nero near their Alpha, I longed to rush over to them. To find out how they'd been. Find out if they missed me as much as I did them. Judas' father, a barbarian of man, stood nearby, studying me, glaring at me. And I doubted he'd appreciate me gushing over his son.

Me, the birthday girl.

With her supposed demon boyfriend.

Shit. I had to talk to Judas, and explain everything.

"Don't think she likes you manhandling her." Ava stepped forward, narrowing her gaze at Thorin, who didn't so much as blink in her direction. He was arrogant son of a bitch.

"You won't push me aside again," he hissed, fire lighting up in his pupils. "After the Reckoning, you'll have your new direction, and we'll get married."

"Whoa." Ava waved her hands about. "You're moving so fast on this, lover boy. She's not into you."

While my go to response to Thorin would normally come in the form of an insult, I couldn't afford that here. Not with so many spectators, without my parents to pick up the pieces. And suddenly, that hard assed responsibility shit they always talked about hit me square in the chest.

*Your actions always have consequences.*

*Take responsibility.*

*Stop behaving like a child.*

Their reprimanding circled my thoughts like vultures.

So, I raised my chin and forced a smile. "I'm so thirsty."

At once, Thorin straightened, and with a final kiss to my hand, he released me. "I'll be right back."

The moment he turned his back to us, Ava and I hurried in the opposite direction.

"What the hell's the deal with that creep?" Ava nudged me then collected two glasses of sparkly and handed me one. "Want me to shank him?"

I cut her a hard stare. "You concealing a blade under that dress?"

"No," she snarled, her gaze a dagger in his back. "But I could be...if you need me to."

Yep, I loved her, and couldn't have asked for a more badass best friend.

"My father thinks our union will help unify the

Vampires and Demons, make us stronger against the Wolf packs."

"Oh." She took a sip of her drink, then wrinkled her nose as if the bubbles tickled her. "He really hates Wolves then, hey?"

He did. A little too much.

I glanced at Judas and felt that surge of friendship, but it was more than that. It was different, deeper, hungrier. I glanced to Nero and Bond behind him, and fought the urge to stride across the room and wrap my arms around them. I wanted to be back there, in that moment where the heady scent of wolf invaded my lungs and we'd held each other...protected each other. But in this moment, the Academy was a million miles away.

The sharp crack of laughter wrenched me from the moment. Nesrin turned to Judas, and murmured something. Trust Dad to invite the cats as well. One wrong move tonight and I'd be a laughing stock for all of eternity.

Her eyes glittered and she acted like she didn't have a care in the world.

But she did.

There was the small unresolved murder of a mortal hovering in the background.

She'd pay...her and her feral friends.

"Come on." I grabbed Ava's hand and turned to the other guests, pasting a smile on my face to nod and welcome everyone who came. Thorin watched me from the edges of the party. Every time our gaze connected I felt my stomach harden. Dad might want one thing for me...but I wanted something completely different.

Hermond was here...the Vamp was kicking it Vlad style again tonight with a black, floor-length cape, only this time he had someone in tow. The female Vamp turned toward me, for a second, I couldn't place her, until our gaze connected. Dark brown, beady looking eyes, pasty pale skin.

It was the Vamp girl from the Academy.

Their bodyguards stood close, all muscle bound brutes with that tell-tale shine of silver in their eyes.

"You know her muscle men are Werewolves," Ava whispered in my ears\. "I thought Vamps and Wolves didn't get along?"

I stared at the towering hulks of canine force and answered. "They don't."

*"Okay, can I have your attention everyone!"*

I turned at Dad's voice. He waltzed in with Mom at his side carrying a large box wrapped in a red ribbon. His black and white tux was stunning, as was the teal, off the shoulder gown Mom wore. They both looked stunning.

"Thank hell," I murmured.

"If we had to make small talk anymore, I was going to slit my wrists," Ava snarled under her breath. "Go see your parents, I'm gonna hang here."

I nodded as she drifted toward Judas, Bond, and Nero. Dad smiled as the crowd turned toward him.

"Dad." I searched his eyes, desperate to draw his gaze. "I need to talk to you,"

He smiled, dark eyes glinting. "I hope you've been keeping everyone company?"

"We need to talk." I glanced toward the others. "Now."

Mom was at my side, drawing me into a hug. "Baby, I'm so proud of you turning one hundred."

"Thanks, Mom," I muttered and wriggled out of her embrace. Dad turned away from me, placing the gift onto the table.

The crowd seemed to spill closer, and I searched frantically over my shoulder for the Ancient. Any moment now, he'd be here, and no doubt he'd bring others just as powerful as he was. The guests closed in around us, and the room felt smaller. Too damn small.

I reached for Dad's arm, clasping it hard. "Please, just give me five minutes outside. It's *important*," I whispered.

He looked down at me, his smile never fading. "Everything has its time, Morwenna. First." He scanned the crowd. "*My gift to you*," he boomed.

Pinching my lips together, my chest tightened, and I wanted to scream at him, drag him outside. But that would draw attention. Then I noticed an Ancient Vampire had sauntered in the room, almost floating rather than walking. He was pale as snow, hair fallen to his shoulders, and gaunt. His cape dragged behind him, and he cut us a dark look.

He gave me the shivers.

Dad took my hand and drew me closer to his gift.

"Come on now. Don't make everyone wait." He stared at me with so much admiration, with love. He meant the world to me. I couldn't lose him, and he had to know.

So, I turned and hugged him and in his ear I whispered, "Someone wants to murder you tonight."

He flinched then pushed me away from him by my shoulders. His serious expression evaporated as fast as it came. "This isn't a time for jokes. Now let's not keep everyone waiting."

Clenching my jaw, I realized that he wouldn't budge, so I'd get this over with, and then I'd drag him aside. I turned to the box and pulled the ribbon. It unraveled, falling to the floor.

"It's said to be the cutest animal on the planet," Dad boasted, staring at everyone but me. "It's a red panda!"

A snarl and a hiss slipped from the box. Whatever was in there didn't sound *cute*.

I hit the latch and the top gave way. Claws the size of daggers speared through the opening and slashed the air. Dad jumped backwards when a head popped up from the open top. Black, beady eyes, and a glistening midnight snout stared at me. The damn thing was ugly as sin. It hissed and snarled, showing more impressive looking teeth.

"Ah, *that thing* is not a red panda," someone called.

Dad was mortified, he stared at the creature and then strode forward, snatching the invoice stuck to the top of the cage. "That's *not* what I ordered."

I caught the logo at the top of the invoice and raise a brow. "Ebay for animals...*really Dad?*"

He frantically muttered, looking at a set of numbers on the box and the ones on the paper.

"That thing is hideous," Nesrin laughed. "Suits you though, Morwenna."

I spun at the savage remark and dragged my hands to my hips. "You know what? It does, it has teeth and claws and *won't* be pushed around. I'm keeping it, Daddy. Thank you for my gift, I love my panda-thingy!"

"Honey badger," Dad corrected. "It's still a baby."

"It's perfect." I reached out to scratch its head, but the damn thing screamed and swiped at me.

Everyone around us ooed and ahhed, except Nesrin who rolled her eyes.

"Before we can really start our celebrations," Father announced, "I graciously welcome our very own Ancient. Vlad Vasile."

The creepy Vamp glided forward like a rolling fog, his dark eyes locked on mine. Everyone stepped out of his path.

He stood alongside me and pulled out a blade from his belt before clearing his throat.

"Child, give me your hand." His voice was like sandpaper, rough and gravelly.

I was hypnotized by those ancient eyes. Stars seemed to sparkle inside them, for a second one twinkled brighter than the others...calling me.

Pain slashed across my palm. "Ouch."

I flinched and tried to jerk my hand back, but the Ancient gripped tight, holding me still as a bead of blood welled in the cut and crested the meat of my palm.

He pressed my hand to his mouth, licking my blood, and I shuddered at his cold, slick tongue. Even Ava cringed, her expression tight. But this was a necessity. A part of the ritual. An Ancient tasted my blood, and with his foresight, dictated where my future lay.

A low hiss slipped from his lips. He jerked his gaze to mine and I was caught by that sparkle again as the star grew brighter.

I waited for the words Dad wanted so desperately to hear, *Theologian*...and tried keep my stomach from dropping to the floor.

"Understudy," the word slipped from the Ancient's lips.

There was a hiss from the crowd.

And then a moan from Dad.

"What did you say?" I murmured.

The Ancient rose to his full height, power rippled through the air. "I name you Understudy to me. You will report to the Great Hall the day after tomorrow, there we will discuss your position."

"Wait," Dad muttered, his frantic gaze finding mine, "there must be some mistake, Sire. You haven't handed out the role of Understudy for thousands of years. Not since the last one...not since the last one went missing."

But the Ancient never looked away, only held my gaze

and murmured. "I think it's time for a little fresh blood, don't you?"

I couldn't speak, only nod my head slowly.

*Understudy.* I didn't even know what that was. All I did know was that it wasn't a calling with my head stuck in a book for the rest of my endless life. "Thank you," I finally murmured. "I will dedicate myself to this role."

"*No!*" Dad snarled.

But there was no undoing what had already been done. The Ancient lowered my hand, his pale lips still glistening red with my blood, and in an instant...he stepped away, watching Dad with interest.

The crowd moved around him, careful not to touch or bump. It didn't matter what breed of immortal you were, when you were in the presence of an Ancient, everyone was on edge.

"I can't believe it," Dad muttered.

Loud, heavy footfalls sounded behind us. "Make way!" a male voice cut through the crowd. "Tricks City Police coming through!"

Dad jerked his head toward the sound as two officers pushed through the crowd, heading toward us. The plain clothed officer gripped a folded piece of paper in his hand. He scanned the crowd, then Dad, and finally stilled on me. "Morwenna Livingston, you are under arrest for suspicion of murder."

# CHAPTER SIXTEEN

## ONE MUST ALWAYS CHEW THEIR FOOD

"What the hell did you say?" I muttered and jerked my gaze to the mortal cop behind me.

Panic raced, tearing along my veins.

Dad's eyes were wide, shining like glass. It was the kind of look I'd seen once before, long ago, in the eyes of a man close to *the killing edge.*

"Daddy, *no,*" I whispered, searching his eyes, desperate to make him see.

This was what they wanted.

This was what they'd bargained for.

*"You're arrested on suspicion of a mortal's murder,"* the officer roared beside me, drawing the attention of everyone around us. "And because this goes against *The Code* of not killing humans, we have the right to detain you for a period of a year to investigate."

"A year?" Dad growled. "I don't think so."

Mom was at my side, her expression petrified, and she collected the badger from my arms.

"Sebastian," the Ancient hissed on the other side.

I turned to Nesrin and her pack of feline bitches, but I

didn't see pride...I didn't see smugness...I saw surprise...I saw confusion and *fear*.

My heart gave a *thud* and then a shudder.

*It wasn't them.*

*It wasn't them who set me up...*

My breath seemed to leave my chest, and for a second none returned.

But movement from the Vampire at Dad's back caught my eyes. Pale lips curled into a sneer, he glanced at me, thin, white fangs sliding over pale lips.

Silver eyes glinted in the bodyguards around Hermond, protecting the young female Vamp at his side.... The girl from the Academy... The one who watched me from the shadows.

It all made sense. Wolf bites covering Vamp ones.

Tainted blood in the vending machines.

And the fact they never came near me...not once, not in the weeks I'd attended Bestias Academy. They didn't like me...she didn't want me here at all, and neither did her father. Hermond didn't just want my father's position in the council...*he wanted him dead.*

Someone screamed in the crowd, and it was like the blast of a starting gun.

Hermond's lips curled from his fangs, his face distorted with rage before he lunged.

Terror drove a fist through my stomach. My eyes dropped to the table in front of me, and the dagger we used for cutlery as I tore out of the mortal cop's grasp. My hand went around the steel, instinct took over.

I wasn't a Vampire in this moment.

Or someone famous.

*I was a daughter.*

I yanked back the blade and whipped it through the air

as Hermond went for my father's throat. The tip of the steel punctured pale flesh, carving right through one side of his mouth and out of the other.

Gunshots rang out as the crowd surged forward. I lost sight of Dad in the stampede, but there was Chuck, towering over everyone screaming, *"Get out of the Goddamn way!"*

The Vampire bodyguard bent, grasped Dad by the arm and then lifted his gaze to me.

"Protect him!" I roared, but my words were lost to deafening boom of shotguns.

Silver eyes flashed. Three sets, as Judas, Nero, and Bond charged through the crowd, leaving their parents behind. Controlled rage lingered in their eyes. Judas lifted his hand and pointed at me. 'We're coming!"

But the human cop behind me was still screaming. "Get back! *Get the Hell back. I'm the Police!"*

Did he realize...badge or no badge...we were the predators, and he was the prey?

"You okay?" Judas voice was a panicked rush in my ear.

I looked over my shoulder to the Vampire bitch in the shadows. "It's her Judas...the Vampire...Hermond's *daughter."*

"Don't worry about that now," Bond snarled as he raced ahead and shoved open the patio door of my home. "We need to make sure you're safe."

*"Morewenna!"* Dad roared behind me as the crowd surged forward, and gunshots followed.

*"Enough!"* An Ancient roared, the air rippling with savage hunger. *"What is the meaning of this!"*

Long standing feuds erupted, Vampires and Wolves, Ghouls and Demons. I saw Thorin as he lunged through the air with a dagger in his hand, and buried it hilt deep into a massive Ghoul's back.

"This isn't right." I clung to Judas. *This is NOT right!*

But Judas never slowed, he raced through the foyer as Nero fell behind.

"Wait for me!" Ava roared behind us.

Gunshots mingled with screams. The party was filled with *mayhem* as Judas rushed through the patio door. The others followed, Ava close behind.

"I have to go back there!" I struggled in Judas' hold. "My Mom...*my Dad.*"

"*They can take care of themselves,*" Judas snapped. "It's you they want, don't you get that?"

"We need to hide." Nero scanned the foyer.

"She fucking did this," I muttered and lifted my hands. "*All of this...for what? Power? Greed?*"

"I *never* liked her," Judas snarled. "That's why the first time I saw you, when we collided in the hallway, I thought you were her."

"I can walk, put me down," I growled.

He lowered my feet to the floor, sucking in hard breaths as he turned to the others. "We have to find a way out of here."

"We fight," Bond growled. "It's the only way...whatever comes through those doors we take on."

I glanced at Ava. She was pale and shaking. "There has to be another way."

Silver eyes flashed through the window. I stumbled backwards as the Vamp girl and her massive Wolf goons raced for the door. "Upstairs!" I roared. "*Now!*"

We turned to the stairs, and all five of us moved, clamouring up each step as the sound of shattering glass filled the foyer.

*"Get them!"* Vamp girl screamed behind us.

The sickening snarls of Wolves crowded in, bouncing against the walls of my home as we reached the first level. Bond and Nero took off in opposite directions. I reached out, grasped Ava's hand and kept on running, taking the stairs two and three at a time. "Come on!"

She stumbled and ran, our heels clattering amongst the hungry growls. There was a brutal *thump,* followed by the crunch of bone. I looked over my shoulder to see Nero and Bond swing at two of the bodyguards.

But they were dwarfed in size. The towering bodyguards barely flinched as Nero and Bond swung, their fists connecting with jaw and ribs. Muscles rippled along their arms as the powerful shifters turned on my protectors.

*"Come on,"* Judas snarled behind me. "They'll hold them off for as long as they can."

*But they'll get hurt.* The words resounded in my head. Pain lashed my chest, but the Alpha at my back kept pushing, driving me upwards, past the second and then the third story. I tore left, toward my bedroom as Judas' hand fell from the middle of my back.

My hands were slick against Ava's, still I grasped her tight and glanced behind me.

But Judas wasn't following, he stood in the middle of stairs, taking one last glance at me before he turned. *No! Please no!*

"Come on," Ava growled, she frantically scanned the hallway before we tore into my room.

There were clothes still scattered on the end of my bed. Open boxes of Armani, soft and flowing, diamonds glinting like fallen stars.

*"We have to hide!"* I roared and looked to my closet. "In there."

But Ava just shook her head. "We'll be cornered."

Judas let out a roar, the sound of fists and grunts followed. They were fighting out there...and we were in here, trying to hide.

I gave a nod and my grip around her relaxed. I turned to her, my friend...the one who'd die fighting with me and gave a nod.

And that merciless killer instinct rose within me once more.

I'd had a taste of my power when the cat gang stole my ring, now it was rising again...like father, like daughter, the killing edge claimed me.

"Get behind me." I tugged her hand.

Grunts and whimpers came from the hallway outside, and was followed by a low, agonized moan. I stopped, staring at the doorway as the echo of heavy steps rang out. I scanned the bedroom, dropping Ava's hand long enough to snatch the brand new pair of stilettos from their box.

They weren't a blade, but they'd do.

Shadows spilled across the doorway as a Wolf stepped into my room.

"I want you to kill them," Vamp girl snarled behind him. "Make it bloody."

"You don't have to do this." I gripped the shoe like a weapon. "I don't even know who you are!"

"That's *precisely* the point," she spat. "All we ever see is *Morwenna Livingstone.* I'm so goddamn sick of your ugly ass face. My daddy is just as powerful, *just* as important, and after tonight...he's gonna be *just as famous.*"

Ugly?

*Who the fuck is she calling ugly?*

"I don't think so."

The deep, trembling snarl didn't sound like Ava at all.

Something glinted in her eyes, something that sent a shiver along my spine. "Ava?"

She never answered, only watched the Wolf and the Vamp step further into the room. Blood covered the Wolf's shirt and there were smears along his cheek. I glanced to the doorway behind him. There was no sound from Judas...or Nero or Bond.

It was just us.

Just us fighting a beast.

The Wolf's lips curled as he stepped closer, his gaze focused on Ava.

"Don't take another step," she warned. "I don't want to hurt you."

Goosebumps raced along my skin. I gripped the heel in my hand. "You want to hurt someone, fleabag? *I'm right fucking here.*"

The Vamp bitch smiled as she strode forward. She reached into her pocket, pulled out a canister and sprayed a steady stream of liquid through the air. The scent of salt filled my nose, before the Vamp bitch jerked the stray toward me.

I ducked, lashing out my hand to cover my eyes.... But Ava just stood there.

"You spray salt water on me?"

The Wolf flanked our side, his gaze caught between me and Ava. I took a step backwards, reaching out to pull my best friend with me.

But she refused to move, only shifted her gaze from the Vamp bitch to her mutt.

"Call off your dog now." Ava's voice was the crash of the sea...hard, *unforgiving.*

Still the Wolf edged closer, taking one more step. And then with an unmerciful *squelch,* something thick and long tore from the dress of my best friend, ripping the spider silk fabric.

Blood red tendrils filled the room, bigger than my damn thigh, stronger than anything I'd ever seen before. And they came from my best friend! They lashed around the Wolf, lifting him into the air with barely more than a sudden breath, and hauled him through the air...*and into her mouth.*

But it wasn't her mouth...it was a beast's *suction* mouth. Rows and rows of razored white teeth chomped and tore.

Fur.

Fangs.

*Fucking everything* was gone.

Holy fuck!

I barely caught sight of the soles of his boots before she swallowed him down. One heavy tendril hit the floor, holding her steady....*as she ate a goddamn Wolf.* The Vamp bitch just stared, wide-mouthed, and then screamed. She lunged, fingers curled into nails, white fangs aiming for my neck.

Tendrils grasped her mid-flight, dragging her toward Ava's greedy mouth. Something growled inside Ava, some-thing more ferocious than anything I'd ever heard before.

My insides turned to water.

My knees trembled as the Vamp girl disappeared the same way as the Wolf.

And in one slow, terrified thud of my heart, we were all alone in my bedroom.

The thick arms of Ava's beast sucked against my floor, leaving slick marks in their wake as they slowly drew back inside her body.

The room was silent.

*We* were silent.

Until I spoke. "You've *got* to be fucking kidding me." I turned toward her, catching the flinch in her eyes.

"You'll hate me now," the small, terrified voice of my best friend broke out.

"Hate you?" I turned toward her, lifting my hand to the empty goddamn room. "Why the *fuck* didn't you do that before? It would've saved us all this fucking hassle."

Her eyes widened as I took a step closer. My heart was thundering, shaking my chest as I wrapped my arms around her. "You saved my life. How can I do anything other than love you...even if you're a little goddamn scary."

"Mor?" Judas moaned from outside.

I pulled away, catching Ava's fear lift with the beginning of a smile.

"You really don't hate me?" she whispered.

I reached for her hand. "I really don't fucking hate you, come on, we've got others to save. First, put on a new dress as you're revealing your wares, girl."

She turned and grabbed the first thing on the bed, and quickly changed into a simple green number that sat on her shoulders from spaghetti straps and reached half-way down her thighs.

I dropped the heel I'd been holding and hurried from the bedroom, falling to my knees as Judas tried to push up against the floor. Blood covered the side of his face. He swayed on his feet, and fell into me. I grasped him under the arms to help him up.

He was a dead weight in my arms, all muscle and gorgeous eyes. *Don't look Mor...don't look into those eyes.* I tried to focus on anything else and bent low enough to grasp him under his knees, before I lifted.

"You're not..." he muttered, horrified.

I glanced at him then, meeting his gaze and smiled. "I am."

And I carried my Wolf in my arms, all the way down the stairs to where Nero and Bond both shook their heads in amusement and grabbed the bannister, hauling themselves to their feet. There were two wolves laying spread out on the floor, neither of them were moving.

I glanced to my protectors. "I'm impressed."

Nero tried to smile but it just looked like a wince. "You should be." He glanced at Judas, whose head rolled back against my shoulder. "How is he?"

"He'll live." I gripped him tighter. "Although he probably won't want to when word gets around his girlfriend had to carry him."

"Girlfriend?" Nero murmured. "Is that so? You know the pack shares right? What's his is ours."

I took a step, striding right past the two of them. "I know... *I was counting on it.*" I should have blushed at my brazen words, but after all the shit we'd faced, I wasn't holding back.

I could have died tonight.

Their steps stilled behind me. I didn't have to turn to see the surprise in their eyes as I carried Judas down to the foyer.

"*Morwenna!*" Dad roared, bursting into the house. He was dripping with blood...as was the rage filled warrior behind him. The dagger in Chuck's hand was coated, the crimson mess had splashed halfway up his arm. But it wasn't me the warrior looked to first...

It was Ava by my side.

"Are you okay?" Dad glanced at the Wolf in my arms, and then the others. "Did they try to hurt you?"

"What? *Dad, no.* They protected me...*they're my friends.*" I eased Judas' feet to the floor as Bond and Nero came up on either side, each taking an arm before they stumbled away.

"The Ancient's are cleaning up the rest," Dad murmured with a wince. "It's a bloodbath out there."

"It was all Hermond and his daughter," I pleaded. "I didn't do any of this. I swear."

"We know," the deep, rolling voice of the Ancient filled the air.

Danger and power followed.

I lowered my gaze, bending one shuddering knee to bow before him. "I'm so sorry," I murmured. "They tried to get me expelled, tried to kill me with tainted blood."

"Is this true?" the Ancient growled. I lifted my gaze as he turned to my father.

"Yes," Dad answered. "Morwenna and her friends were attacked, it's why we bought her home."

"But we protected her," Ava murmured in a small voice. She glanced to the Wolves. "We *all* protected her."

The Ancient just looked at her, taking in her eyes, her blonde hair. He took a step and I caught Ava flinch. "You...you smell of the sea, strong, *powerful.* You remind me of someone. Someone I knew long ago."

He stepped backwards, cutting me a careful glance. "You will remain at this Academy, along with your friends for now. But you will report to me before nightfall tomorrow, and we will start your training as my understudy."

"My Lord." There was a tremor in my father's voice. "I don't think she's strong enough for such a position—"

The Ancient Vampire cut him off with a wave of his hand, dark, bottomless eyes searching mine as he answered. "Maybe not yet...but she will be."

And he turned, sliding along the floor with barely a sound, leaving us standing alone.

"I'll make sure the Ancient is safe to leave," Chuck growled as he turned away, striding for the shattered patio door.

"I think I'll do the same," Ava muttered and hurried after him.

Dad just looked at me. There was so much he wanted to say in his gaze. But in the end, all he did was lean close and murmur. "Those two are going to be a problem, aren't they?"

My eyes widened. I glanced at Ava as she called out. "Chuck, *youuuwhooo*. Wait up!"

"Yes," I answered watching my awkward, weirdass...best goddamn friend run after the warrior. "Yes...they are."


Can't get enough of Manicures and Mayhem? Want an extra scene written just for you? Click here to find out what happened when the Wolves and Ava went to get Mor's ring.

It's Kila Foung here.

We tried to warn you.
We really did...
We hope you liked Manicures and Mayhem. The good
news is, there's a lot more where this came from...the bad
news is also...there's a lot more where this came from.
Dammit...
We're fucking begging for Ava and Chuck to have their
moment, and we need you to band with us. PLEASE tell up
how hard you ship these two right now.

And the Wolves??? What the Hell...we want more...a lot
more.
And we hope you do too.

Love crazy eyes and kissy face...aka Kila Foung

DIAMONDS AND DEMONS